WE ALL
BELONG

**Mission Center**
826 Valencia Street
San Francisco, CA 94110

**Tenderloin Center**
180 Golden Gate Avenue
San Francisco, CA 94102

**Mission Bay Center**
1310 4th Street
San Francisco, CA 94158

826valencia.org

Published May 2019 by 826 Valencia
Copyright © 2019 by 826 Valencia

The views expressed in this book are the authors' and do not necessarily reflect those of 826 Valencia. We support student publishing and are thrilled that you picked up this book!

**Program Manager and Editor**
Ryan Young

**Editorial Assistants**
Dana Belott, Alexandra Cotrim, Geordi Galang, Kiana Lew, Olivia Mertz

**Editorial Board**
*Volunteer Editors* Susannah Cohen, Geordi Galang, Cristina Giner, Eric Hendrickson, Maura Kealey, Caroline Moon
*Student Editors* Kevin G., Florante M., Jaedyn N., Elizabeth W., Caiyan Y.

**Volunteer Tutors**
Asifuzzaman Ahmed, Scott Andersen, Randie Bencanann, Paolo Bicchieri, Lindsey Bourne, Brittany Carrico, Susannah Cohen, Alexandra Cotrim, Lila Cutter, Shelby Dale DeWeese, Mag Dimond, Ashley Escobar, Cassidy Fix, Joel Fruchtman, Ana Fuentes, Geordi Galang, Cristina Giner, Anna Griffin, Zoey Haar, Eric Hendrickson, Michael Huggins, Mio Ikeda, Maura Kealey, Elizabeth Kert, Daniel Mclaughlin, Caroline Moon, Eric Mueller, Courtney Norman, Daniel Raskin, Ann Ryles, Akbarkhanzadeh Saam, Tish Scola, Angelina Sideris, Michele Sloat, Anne Sloper, Laura Smyrl

**Partner Teachers**
K.R. Morrison and Jennifer Stangland

**Design Director**
Brad Amorosino

**Publications Manager**
Meghan Ryan

**Designer**
Molly Schellenger

**Illustrator**
Lisa Congdon

**Copyeditor**
Beret Olsen

ISBN 978-1-948644-33-4
Printed in Canada by Prolific Graphics
Distributed by Ingram Publisher Services

# WE ALL BELONG

—

**Reflections about borders from the
students of Galileo High School
With a foreword by Luis J. Rodriguez**

# TABLE OF CONTENTS

—

## IN BETWEEN

—

# FOREWORD:
# ULTIMATELY, WE ALL BELONG
—

## LUIS J. RODRIGUEZ

Today Mexican and Central American refugees are being lied about, discriminated against, detained, and torn from their families in a country founded on freedom, rights, and equality. The gap between the ideal and the real is vast—mostly because it has taken 230 years or more to expand these rights to all peoples on this land: women, Native Americans, African Americans, Mexicans, Puerto Ricans, poor whites, immigrants, Muslims, LGBTQ, and more. That is the aim—the direction of which is full and irrevocable equity for all.

We have a long way to go. However, nothing helps us more on this road than hearing the voices of young people who are the most affected by the empties and cracks in the body politic. The stories included here are from youth whose families have roots in Nicaragua, Guatemala, China. They talk about the simple things—mother love, one's village, the trees and fruits one remembers, a cemetery, the produce market, even the local McDonald's. But they also write about the dangerous things, like crossing more than one border, each more perilous than the previous, to get to the border of all borders: that of the United States. The end of the line for most people. Trying to find a better life for oneself, one's family and friends is a longtime human endeavor. Migration has been going on for tens of thousands of years. In these voices, you get to imagine the songs, the fears, the pains, but also the joys and triumphs.

In the end, Mother Earth, Father Sky, and all the cosmos don't care about borders, or what language one speaks, or how much wealth one may have. We all belong just by being human.

We need more voices and stories like these.

# IN THE SAME SOIL

—

# INTRODUCTION

—

## JENNIFER STANGLAND
*ENGLISH TEACHER AT GALILEO HIGH SCHOOL*

Today's youth face a harsh reality—a reality that renders many of their voices muted, their influences dampened, and their insights left undiscovered. This harsh reality is the fact that, regardless of what they are *told* regarding the supposed importance of their voices, influence, and insight, youth are often never truly *empowered*. How often do student voices actually make it beyond the classroom or their peer groups? How often are their stories read by someone other than their teacher? How often are our communities, our cities, and our countries meaningfully molded by those we consider the shaping force of our future?

As an educator, I am confronted with this reality almost daily. I see the faces of students who have rich experiences and complex understandings of our world, yet rarely have a venue by which to bring that knowledge to the world. Perhaps the most unfortunate component of this reality is that students *feel* it. They know when they are not heard; they know when their contributions in a classroom never move beyond its walls; they know when their life experiences are not considered valid. Yes, the goal of education is to prepare youth to effectively use knowledge to influence their futures; however, aren't we missing a great resource in the present?

My students have stories to share. Their stories are powerful, raw, creative, and often move me to tears. This is exactly why they needed to write this book. These young men and women experience borders in their lives that I could never imagine, understand the beauty and tragedy of family in unique ways, and have the power to provide a window into other worlds for those of us who will listen.

826 Valencia has given the great gift of empowerment to these young lives, and for that, I am beyond thankful. The laughter, creativity, and newfound confidence these young writers exuded as they composed their stories is proof that they *feel* that gift. My hope is that this compilation of stories will echo across ears, minds, hallways, classrooms, conversations, cities, and maybe even countries, not stopping until it has inspired other young voices to join its reverberating rhythm of expression.

# UNTITLED

—

## BOSHARA A.

Dear Diary,

~~It's me, Boshara, but you already know me.~~ I'm still stuck. It's been a couple weeks since I've drawn ~~something.~~ ~~I just feel like I physically can't pick up the pencil or paint and just start.~~ ~~I had this one idea but~~ I feel like I~~, Boshara A., just~~ can't perfect it. My painting ~~idea~~ is ~~of a bunch of the same fish in the sea, but one of the fish~~ is a ~~different color—~~ ~~making it stand out. It's~~ supposed to capture the feeling of being lonely, yet surrounded by a sea of people. ~~A feeling of being different from the others.~~

~~I love this idea,~~ but I don't feel like I can do it. ~~I feel like someone else deserves to paint this more than I do, even though it's my idea.~~ Maybe ~~it's 'cause~~ I keep doubting myself ~~and my ability. I keep thinking about this a lot. I spend so much time putting myself down that~~ I start losing motivation. ~~I like to have a precise time, preferably hours, to draw, or I'll usually start forgetting about it and end up never finishing.~~ I don't know why ~~I feel this pressure,~~ but it is a big push down.

Everyone loves my art ~~pieces,~~ but ~~I can't seem to myself.~~ I ~~will~~ always find something ~~to point out~~ that ruins it. I ~~tend to~~ compare my art to other people's. ~~It's a bad habit, and~~ I should stop, but I ~~really~~ can't. ~~I guess it's a way to keep in check.~~

~~I have so much on my mind that I just start eliminating my options~~ ~~until I have no more. So, by the time I pull out the small white canvas,~~ my mind is blank. ~~Sometimes~~ I just can't ~~use this small mind of mine.~~ ~~I'll have an idea, but I can't~~ imagine how it'll look, so I just quit. ~~What~~ ~~can I say? I don't tend to quit much, but when I do it's~~ because I've been trying for so long.

~~Not only does it affect me emotionally, but physically, too. I don't take~~ ~~art classes because~~ I don't want to lose. ~~I know that~~ every winner loses, but I can't do it. ~~I also know that I can't win~~ if I don't try, ~~but if I don't try~~ nothing bad can happen. ~~So I'll just stay where I'm at. One thing I know~~ ~~for sure is that I'm a professional when it comes to watching Netflix, so . . .~~ ~~there really isn't a problem here. Unlike art, Netflix never does me wrong~~ ~~except when the subscription ends, but other than that it's been good.~~

Love,
Boshara A.

———

*Boshara A.* *was born in a house in a small village in Yemen. She moved to San Francisco and has been there her whole life. She is fifteen years old. She is fascinated by works of art on paper, canvas, or body, and the stories they tell. She loves primary colors and bright clothing. She hopes to go all over the world when she gets older, but she really wants to go to underrated European places and watch the northern lights. She went to eight schools overall and wants to go to UC Merced for college. She likes singing and hopes to move away from San Francisco and hopefully, California.*

# DON'T TRUST ANYBODY

—

## MELINA A.

It was my first day of middle school. As I looked around, I saw a bunch of people I had never seen before. I knew nobody. It was 7:30 in the morning. It was cold. I was sitting in the yard. I looked around and saw everyone playing. I saw a girl with long black hair wearing black leggings, a white shirt with a jean jacket, and bright yellow shoes. She approached me and said, "Hi, my name is Adriana. What's your name?" After that day, she became my best friend. Me and Adri were best friends for three years. We told each other everything. We knew each other's deepest, darkest secrets. We told each other everything from what we did over the weekend, to who we liked or who we didn't like. She was like a sister to me.

## "We knew each other's deepest, darkest secrets."

Our school had three floors. The first one was for offices, the second one was for the eighth graders, and the third one was for the sixth and seventh graders. It was passing period as I was walking down the hall full of kids to get to my fifth period class. I saw Adri talking to this girl named Karla. I found that weird because I remember Adri telling me that she never really liked Karla. The next day my friend Nati told me that when she was walking home, she saw Adri and Karla talking at the front of the school. She heard Karla say, "OMG, Melina is so annoying."

Then Adri said, "I know, right? I can't stand her. She doesn't shut up."

And Karla responded, "I know. She was texting me last night about the boy she likes. I keep trying to ignore her."

Adri was like, "She's always talking about her parents and how they're always fighting. Also, she won't stop talking about this guy she likes," as she rolled her eyes and snapped her gum.

Later that day I was walking to the bus stop. It was hot and the sun was in my eyes, so I couldn't really see if it was Adri standing there. As I got closer, I saw that it was Adri and Karla. On the way home, I couldn't help but wonder if they were talking about me. When I got home, Nati sent me a pic of Adri and Karla talking about me without me even asking. When I opened it, my heart dropped. I realized Nati was a good friend.

After I stopped talking to Adri, she and Karla became best friends. They kept starting rumors about me, about how I am fake and that I am always trying to get people's attention and whatnot. I could see the people staring at me as I walked down the hall and they were pointing at me and laughing. That made me feel so sad and made me think I really couldn't trust anybody, because even the people you're closest to can hurt you.

After that, I realized that I put a wall up, meaning I wouldn't trust anybody and it was harder for me to make friends. I always thought that someone was trying to hurt me. That border wasn't just for friends, it was for people in general. I trusted nobody.

It's been three years since that happened. I'm still very careful about who I talk to. I have my best friend that I tell everything to. We have been friends for two years. Because of her, I can somewhat trust people. I don't tell people my business, but I have started to open up more and try to be more friendly, even if I try to stay alone.

Yes, I have my school friends—they are on my border. I also have my boyfriend, and he has passed my border. It's hard to tell him how I feel and whatnot because of my trust issues, but I think it's getting easier to trust him and other people. In the future, I can see myself opening up, trusting people, and having more friends, but as of right now, I think it's best if I keep things to myself.

———

*Melina A.* *is from Ecuador. She is fifteen and is going to be sixteen on August 22. She has two brothers—one older, and one younger. Her favorite food is wings.*

# WHAT IS A BORDER TO YOU?

—

## MARWAN A.

SURPRISED. A moment when I noticed that there was a border or something that stopped me was when I planned the day out, but then my friends were stopped by their parents or changed their minds. A border can be there in two ways: one, a permanent border, or two, a border that can be passed. In this story, the border is permanent because plans were canceled and plans were over, so the day became a waste, but tomorrow will be a new day, so plans could go successfully.

BACKGROUND. Before I go out with my friends, I'm usually still at home, so I'm with my family. My dad goes on the sofa, my mom is in the kitchen, my siblings are on their electronics, and I'm lying down in bed on my phone. It sounds like games, cars, news, and more because my siblings are playing on their electronics. The frame on the wall holds a picture of family during Eid. Eid is a religious holiday for Muslims. The home smells like baked bread. Every day this is a routine, although sometimes we go out as a family. This is the schedule for the weekdays.

HOPE. My friends are at home while I'm planning. They play games while I'm working on what to do. My friends and I always hang out and see what we should do in the Tenderloin. We always want to leave the area and always go somewhere else because the TL is really dirty with a lot of homeless people on the sidewalks. The block where we live has a lot of drug dealing. I see homeless people sticking needles into their arms and poop everywhere. I used to be scared in the area, and many people who don't live around here are scared. I got used to it by walking every day and seeing what's going on, which is kind of sad because it used to be a good neighborhood, but now it's dangerous. What I do to stop the people from taking drugs is act like I am recording, and they get shy and don't stick the needles in their arms. I see the blood drip down to the sidewalk, pouring into the drain. I smell fresh blood and can taste blood. It's just dirty and there are many bad situations, like car crashes, hit-and-runs, and fights. So, we go somewhere else clean and nice, like Mission Bay. I hope I can overcome this situation most of the time.

JOY. On weekends we have more time than on weekdays, so in the morning we text in groups about what we should do that day. This happens a lot of the time when the weekend is here.

PRESSURE. Planning feels like pressure because I plan and then it doesn't happen and I get bored. I feel angry because my friends change their minds. It's not right for my friends to say that they are coming and end up changing their minds. I feel like I wasted time and think about how fun it could've been, so I feel like I missed out because that day went to waste. The reason why I'm complaining is because I have wasted many days in the past.

TRUST. Parents and children need to gain trust to know where the children actually go, so the parents can give them more time to be outside. This is how I feel in general about parents and children and how they are. My friends and I go to this place in Mission Bay. It's a University of California, San Francisco gym that has a lot of activities like basketball, pool, exercise, etc. My friends and I just go to swim. It has an outdoor and indoor swimming pool. We go to the indoor pool because it gets cold in the outdoor pool. The border here is some of the parents are worried, so they don't let their children go. My friends' parents get worried because we get home late and it's far. Friends can gain trust by being good people, getting good grades, coming back on time, and being respectful.

ANTICIPATION. Usually friends can be broke or just lazy and that stops us from going there. We are around ninth to eleventh grade, a small group with five friends including me. We also talk about what to get.

"What kind of food do you guys want?" I ask.

"Indian food!" everyone shouts.

We get food a lot of the time and try different foods. Sometimes we argue about what food to get, but sometimes we are feeling like eating the same thing.

Another way plans can be stopped is when my parents stop me from going, or my friends' parents are not letting them go. They stop them as if they are cops and we just robbed the bank. The challenge here is that my friends can't go because their parents won't let them. As you can see, borders can happen quickly without knowing that you got stopped.

"Do you think the world will be like this forever, or will there be a change to make the world peaceful?"

PERSISTENT. Another way to define a border is something physical that is forever. For example, the borders between Mexico and the U.S. People suffer when parents and children are separated. A border is sometimes necessary, so that's how life is. Remember there are borders that can be overcome, but there are borders where it's tough. Do you think the world will be like this forever, or will there be a change to make the world peaceful? Most of the borders are similar, which is why they just get stopped and parents don't want them to go.

HOPE. This story matters because it's about a time where there is a border which comes and leaves. What I mean by that is it comes randomly and it can disappear. Borders that are temporary can be passed. A border is an invisible wall that stops you from doing something, which can be permanent or passed. For example, I couldn't plan anymore because my friends changed their minds or another issue happened. This expression of hope is what the story needs most because sometimes the plans go badly, so all we do is hope for the best.

SUCCESS. The present can be hard, but the future will be easier when I find a successful job.

———

*Marwan A.* *was born in San Francisco. He is sixteen years old. Marwan and his family like to travel a lot. He loves to exercise and write in a journal. His favorite sport is soccer. His goal is to become a safety engineer for cars. He is hardworking and never gives up.*

# OVERCOME

—

## JACOB C.

Leo was born and raised in China. At nine-and-a-half years old, he lived with his grandma, dad, mom, and brother in a cramped apartment with three bedrooms, one bathroom, and a living room connected to a kitchen, but never felt comfortable in it. Leo never liked the feeling of being in cramped places, kind of like being locked in a coffin. So, whenever he could he would leave his apartment, go up the emergency stairs making sure no one saw him, and go out the door onto the roof. He would sit on the edge, holding onto the rail, and embrace the feeling of not being trapped. For hours he would sit, thinking about climbing. Leo loved climbing things, like the emergency ladder on the side of the building, or the trees at the front of the apartment building. But all he really wanted was to be free, free to run anywhere, climb anywhere, not to be trapped in a tiny apartment. And his parents even had well-paying jobs too, but to them this apartment was perfect for their family of five. But one day, his dream came true.

Leo's family had decided to move to San Francisco, as both his parents were offered well-paying jobs there. His mom was offered to be a mechanical engineer at Tesla by showing her fascination and effort in making machines, and his dad was offered to be an Apple mechanical engineer because he could think of good ideas. They moved to Mission Bay in a two-story house with two bathrooms, five bedrooms, and a separate kitchen and living room. This house had a lot of empty space, since their apartment had way fewer things compared to the new home. They lived on one side of the long narrow street that separated the two rows of houses. It was just a long row of houses, and Leo was fascinated. He had always lived in an apartment and had never seen houses side by side instead of on top of each other. But there was one thing that Leo was the most excited about. When moving their belongings into the house, he saw a window, and through that window Leo saw something that he had never seen before.

Leo propped up a stool against the wall and climbed up. Through the window he saw a grassy area with trees, bushes, some flower patches, and an old baby slide that was caked in dirt and was missing a few steps. He was thrilled. He quickly ran around the house looking for a door that led into the backyard. He barely knew this new house, so he opened the front door and the bedroom door thinking that it led to the backyard. Eventually he went downstairs and found a big brown door with a dead bolt on the top half of the door. Leo had seen this before, but wasn't tall enough to unlock it. There wasn't anything to prop against the door to climb up, so he took out the foam football in his pocket that he used to entertain himself on the way to their new home and chucked it at the dead bolt. And, magically, that worked, and it unlocked. Leo turned the doorknob and stepped into this new world.

Leo was thrilled to explore this new land and climb the trees, hide in bushes, go down the slide, and pretend that he was Bear Grylls and survive in the wild. But he noticed something that he hadn't noticed before when he was looking through the window. He found that he was surrounded by a gray chain-link fence on all sides. Almost immediately he felt his claustrophobia enclosing him, making him fidget and sweat from his palms. He could see through the fence, but the feeling remained. Back when Leo lived in his old house, his brother would take leftover cardboard boxes and throw them on top of him and trap him inside. His brother knew of his condition, but still continued to annoy him. But Leo wanted to overcome his condition. Leo knew what he needed to do.

He pushed the old baby slide against the fence, climbed up, and held a firm grip on the chain fence. He lifted himself up and placed a foot in one of the hole squares of the fence. He used all his strength to try and pull himself up, but he only had the strength of a nine-year-old. He couldn't pull himself up the rest of the way. But Leo didn't want to give up. He had a new plan. He pushed the baby slide to the closest tree and climbed onto a thick branch. He slowly inched toward the end of the branch like a tightrope walker. He finally made it to the end and stepped onto the top of the fence, balancing himself with hanging branches making sure he didn't fall off. But nothing happened. He was still fidgeting. He didn't feel the feeling of being on top of the apartment roof. So, he slowly inched his way on the fence toward the house. Four minutes later of slowly inching, he reached the house.

On the side of the house there was a window porch for potted flowers that hung over the sidewalk. He slowly stepped onto it, being careful not to break or step on any plants or plant pots. Then he saw it—a pipe around fifteen inches, two feet away from him, that led up to the roof. Leo knew there was no other way. He grabbed the pipe, using the wedges holding the pipe to climb up. Finally, he reached the top and pulled himself up. On the roof, he looked down to see how high it was, only to see that he would probably get seriously injured if he fell.

He slowly crept toward the front of the house, making sure to stay near the middle of the roof. His apartment building had railings. This one didn't. Two minutes later, he made it to the front of the house and sat down on the edge. He took a deep breath of freedom, not enclosed by the fence anymore. He stood up and took in the view around him. He could see rows and rows of houses, on the other side of the street, too. He turned around and saw his neighbors' backyards too. He was eager to explore this new world. Back in his apartment all he had been able to see were tall buildings and small shops covering the bottom. He had all this place to explore to himself, kind of like his little secret. Leo couldn't wait to explore this, he thought he might even start exploring the jungle in his backyard that day! Just as he thought this, he heard the yell of his dad, "Leo, where are you! We need help taking the boxes in and making our beds for tonight!" Leo had to obey, of course, if he didn't want his family finding his little secret. So, he hurriedly climbed down the pipe, jumped off the fence, and ran inside the house just in time as his dad walked down the stairs.

"Hey, Dad," Leo said, clearly out of breath.

"Where have you been, Leo? You were supposed to help us unpack!" Leo's dad exclaimed.

"I've been, uhh, playing football with myself!" Leo claimed.

"Okay...come on, we need some help getting the TV in," Leo's dad said.

Leo hurriedly ran to the front door, hoping his dad wouldn't investigate anymore. He ran to help his mom with the TV with his dad right behind him.

When unpacking their items Leo thought to himself, *if I can get out of there, even with me being a nine-year-old, then there's always a way out. You don't have to stay trapped.*

---

**Jacob C.** *was born in San Francisco. He is fifteen years old. He loves to play video games and hang out with friends. Jacob loves tech and wants to work at a tech company one day, but doesn't know what position.*

# COMMUNICATION
—

## KATRINA D.

The silence in the room was deafening. I could hear the sounds of the environment so distinctly—the cars driving by, fish splashing in the tank, curtains blowing in the wind, the refrigerator buzzing. It was so quiet, I could feel myself sinking into the couch. It was so comfortable, and also so protective. Even picking up the remote, just sitting there two feet away, felt like a thousand-mile trek. The barrier between us was powerful—the wall was building up, brick by brick.

My parents and I moved in with my grandma because her place was closer to my new school. The silence between us was immediate. Every time we tried to talk, we couldn't understand each other because she solely spoke Mandarin, and I spoke Cantonese or English. It was two dialects from the same country, yet it felt like the earth between us. Whenever we sat near each other, no one was talking. I felt awkward.

One afternoon, my grandma and I were sitting there. I was on my phone, and we could not communicate with each other because of the lack of shared language. We couldn't communicate with each other when we went to restaurants, events, stores, etc. One time, we went to a Chinese restaurant and the workers there spoke both dialects of Chinese. My grandma pointed to the photo of the food that she wanted to tell me about. We used hand gestures to indicate what food we both wanted to order. We still couldn't understand each other and that made me feel like a cloud was between us. The road of thick fog remained the same for half of my life. It didn't just happen at the Chinese restaurant, it happened everywhere else we went.

Back at home, the silence returned and I could hear the world again. The lack of words between us turned the volume on my inside thoughts to a maximum. I would turn on the TV to create sound in the room to distract from the noise of my inner thoughts. I eventually didn't want to communicate. When it was just the two of us at home, it was lifeless. It was so quiet I could hear my heart beating, yet it was also as if both of our hearts had stopped.

# "We still couldn't understand each other and that made me feel like a cloud was between us. The road of thick fog remained the same for half of my life."

Then my family would arrive home at night and the border started to dissolve. It was like an iceberg melting. Their presence provided windows to look through the border, where I could see more clearly. I immediately felt less alone and less awkward. When I came home, there was complete silence while she was sitting by the door watching me come in.

When my mom came home, she said, "Hi, I'm back."

"Hi, what have you bought?" Grandma replied.

"I got this dress for $25. What a great deal, right?" Mom said. The communication continued.

When my uncle came home, Grandma said, "How was work today?"
"It was good," and the conversation continued.

There was communication between my family and my grandma, my family to me, but never my grandma and me. We never had a full conversation between both of us, except for with my family. It was like a bouncy ball bouncing off each other, but it never got to my grandma and me. Every time I came back home, there was no conversation between us. However, when my family came home, there was some kind of greeting.

In summary, my grandma and I didn't communicate much, leading me to not know much about her background. Therefore, I didn't know much about her, such as the origin of my family traits. Now I know that my mom talks a lot because my grandma does. I hope learning more about my grandma can teach me more about myself.

One day, my mom registered me for Mandarin class at a Chinese school on the weekends because she thought learning another language was significant and could help me in the future. My mom's cousin and relatives mostly spoke Mandarin so when they came over we didn't communicate much. I was willing to go to Chinese school even though I didn't know what to expect. I was nervous because I knew what a challenge it would be to learn a whole new language, but all my fears were cast aside when I realized what I was gaining. I was learning communication skills that I never thought I'd need. Learning Mandarin allowed me to gain confidence while talking to others and it has opened many opportunities for me.

The biggest discovery of all was I could start communicating with my grandma. It took me a while, but I started to understand what my grandma was saying. I learned about her relatives, cousins, childhood, adolescent years, schooling, marriage, jobs that she experienced, and much more. It blew my mind into pieces when my grandma unveiled how many relatives and cousins that I never knew I had. She filled in pieces of my ancestry puzzle, and it has shocked me that I never knew over the years that she had so many cousins and relatives that are a part of her life.

Now I feel like there are a lot of people in the world that I never met including my grandma's relatives and cousins. Now that I discovered more about my grandma, it has opened the pathways of cousins and relatives that I never realized I had. Before we shared a language, we didn't talk. Now we do. This has changed our relationship from a quiet surrounding to a bigger world. Now we can communicate without having the feeling of awkwardness. When I am home, the room is constantly filled with voices from two of us.

---

*Katrina D. was born in San Francisco, California and is fifteen years old. She has one sister. She loves to watch YouTube videos such as Daily Life Vlogger. Her favorite color is purple. One day, she hopes to be a pharmacist. In her free time, she likes spending time with friends and family.*

# THE SIGNIFICANT BARRIER

—

## WILLIAM F.

I was tired from the long basketball practice, which had finished just ten minutes before. I was one stop away from my house, on the 30 bus, and couldn't wait to get some rest at home. After I got off the bus, I walked toward my house, not knowing what was about to go down. When I eventually got closer to my corner, I was bombarded with a nauseating smell that destroyed my nostrils, but not really. As I mini-gagged, I thought to myself, *what is that disgusting stench?*

I knew something was off about the street that day and I scanned the area around me, looking for the cause of the smell. While searching, I saw my building which was painted black and white, with many individual houses that were all mixed into one big complex. There was a fake cable car parked on the side of the road, with giant wheels and an engine that gave away that it was a fake cable car. Then I saw him, the smell, the person who made the horrible stink.

He had baggy clothes on, dirty rags hanging on his head. He carried ripped bags, and was covered in dirt all over his body. As I got closer to him, I took in a huge breath and tried not to think about it. Out of nowhere, the homeless man tried to input a code into the keypad that opened up the main gate. I assumed that he was looking for a place to stay, somewhere to shelter himself, maybe between the many dumpsters that sit on the side of the building. He was probably looking for food and trying to stay safe and warm from San Francisco's bipolar weather. As I was watching him try desperately to punch in the right code, I thought of the barrier between us, the wealth gap. He seemed homeless, having nowhere to go, while I had a home and a family that took care of me. In a few years, I could be in a good college playing basketball for them, while he could still be finding a place to call home.

As I walked past him, I kept my cool and tried not to make eye contact. I didn't want to let him into the building by going through the front gate, so I headed for the back gate. When I finally got past him, I gasped for a breath of fresh air. I went through the back gate, walked up the stairs, unlocked the door to my house, and fell onto my couch in the living room.

"There was also a major difference in our opportunities for the future, because I was still young and still learning, while he was just getting by, day to day."

After I went home, I took a short nap to regain my energy, then got my ball, and went back outside to put up some shots at the YMCA's basketball court. Right when I was about to head out, I remembered the man outside the main gate, just waiting there. I approached the main gate and scouted the area around there. He was nowhere to be found, and I walked through the front gate without alarm.

Even though my path through the gate wasn't difficult, I had continuing thoughts in my mind, *what if he managed to get into the building? What if he notifies more homeless men and they try to invade all together? Did he have a purpose being in our specific apartment building?* These questions were stuck in my mind and made me realize that I was fortunate that I had a place to call home and family members who cared about me.

———

**William F.** *was born in China and moved to San Francisco very early on in his life. He likes to play basketball and make new friends. He is on the basketball team and likes to watch the NBA. William also likes every type of food because he wants to try new things.*

# VUELA
—

## GENNESIS G.

### Mom's Story

As a young girl in Nicaragua, all you hear is, "Los estados son muy bonitos y hay muchas oportunidades para trabajar y salir adelante." Comalapa, the village you grew up in, the smallest town there is in Nicaragua, cars barely passing by; everyone knows everybody. The house your parents built from the ground with mango and jocote trees surrounding it. The touch of the grape-sized fruit, mamoncillo, once you bite on the shell with your teeth and it easily opens and you just enjoy. The frijoles and freshly made quesillos, the cuajada, everything just exploded with flavor, the milk from the cow still warm. Being one out of twelve kids, three of your siblings already making their lives out there where you aspire to be. Seeing them becoming so financially stable and living their best lives just makes it so tempting to just go.

*Mi linda Nicaragua cuanto te adoro pero tengo que seguir mis sueños.*

### Pa's Story

Guatemala, unbearable heat, sun hitting your skin, slowly melting you and making you feel like you can't breathe at times, beach just across the block filled with people during *Semana Santa,* when people gathering from many different places in Guatemala just to enjoy the weather and the cold ocean water. Sure, Milton G. had the life in Champerico, being able to go where he wanted when he wanted, helping his father collect the milk from the udders of the many cows they had. But he knew there was more. He had this motivation, and that was his mother. Throughout his youth, this woman who he so vividly remembered, this sweet caring mother of seven, the one that made him who he is up to this day, was thousands of miles away with his older sisters who kept convincing him that it'd be better if he was with them and telling him that the jobs over there were so much easier than the ones in Guatemala. He was a teenager. Who wouldn't want to be with their mother, your nurturer? It was in his nature to be with her no matter what happened. He just needed his mother's love.

**Border, Border, Border**
*You're in my mind, you're in my mind*
*Preventing families from being together*
*Borders—in my mind, you intimidate me*
*I am not able to be myself because of you*
*The pain you have brought me and my family*
*The separation*
*Everything*
*You ruin*
*It's not fair*
*We are all human*
*What is the difference*
*Between me and an upper-class person*
*I am just looked at wrongly*
*Others are not*
*Border, you do not protect*
*You harm*
*And DISCRIMINATE*
*It's a shame to think that*
*This society is such a wreck*
*Every day I am targeted*
*I'm scared*
*Afraid*

## Ma's Story

Fifteen, naive, *"Quiero ser aprobada para la visa."* Eventually, she convinced her mother to take her to Managua, the capital of Nicaragua, Chontales. This teenage girl who had high hopes, going into the Office of National Services, looking at all the faces that surrounded her, the sight of her mother with a glimmer in her eyes. Terrified of what might happen, the first step Raquel took into that office would eventually be the last. After filling out tremendous amounts of paperwork, they went home on a three-hour bus ride, smelling the *tajadas* that people made, watching the people selling Coca-Cola in small bags with a straw, the men hanging onto the bus for dear life just to get somewhere. The bus was always full, but women and children always got seats. Raquel was just happy to at least try and pursue the American Dream. Eventually, about three weeks later, some mail came in and there it was: *"Visa para Raquel Miranda."* She cried the moment she saw her name. It was just astonishing to imagine herself going there. The next day, her mother bought her a one-way ticket to San Francisco, and that was that. She packed her bags, got on that plane knowing her siblings were waiting for her on the other side, and imagined the possibilities for her future.

## Pa's Story

Milton G., determined, taking risks. This seventeen-year-old boy who worked for hours to pay a *"Lobo,"* someone who guaranteed that he'd make it possible for him to get across the border. Although it was $1,500 to pay the guy, Milton was just desperate to get to where his mother was. She was his safe haven. Even if he did have everything in Guatemala, it didn't matter. All he wanted to do was leave and make it out to the States. It didn't matter if he was going to work overtime, the scourging pains that he had after work, the feeling of scorching heat from the vicious sun rays that would burn his back and get him all sunburned from working in fields (and all he could do was put ice on it because he couldn't afford any medicine). Throughout about two or three months, he finally got the money he needed. It was time. My father, *mi pa*, packed up as much as he could and just started going and going as if it was never ending. But at last he got to the border, the most intense and startling moment, and he was afraid. He always thought to himself, *what am I going to do if I don't make it across?* His heart fired up, *inferno*, pulsating uncontrollably. He just prayed to God and went on with the plan. *"No te preocupes, estás en buenas manos,"* the man taking him across said to him with such a confidence that my dad calmed down. They ended up going toward a very sketchy trail filled with cactuses, and if one poked you, it'd feel like a knife was stabbing you, and the only way to make the pain stop was by pulling it out, although you'd start bleeding uncontrollably. This wasn't your ordinary trail, it was one of those trails that as a kid you would never go near—the one with dead trees, the one you avoided the most. At last, he was across and he knew this because the man said to him, *"Ya estás en Los Estados Unidos. Felicidades hermano."* That was that, he got onto a Greyhound bus in a town nearby and headed to San Francisco.

**Me, Myself, and I**

*I am now a Sophomore at Galileo*
*There are pieces in my life that make me complete*
*My entire life is ahead of me*
*The wonders of my future*
*The people who opened doors for me*
*I am my own person*
*I have borders, but I overcome them easily*
*This beautiful soul*
*This amazing mind*
*This, this is who I am*
*I have troubles like any other person*
*And yet I am different*
*My state of mind*
*Everything, it's just unbelievable*

**Ma's Story**

*"Estoy en San Francisco,"* she said as the plane started to slowly get onto the runway. There were no words to describe how she felt— everything was so surreal. She was just excited to finally be here. As she walked out and grabbed her luggage and found her family, the people that she hadn't seen in years brought tears to her eyes. Everyone was overjoyed.

**Pa's Story**

After a good long trip, he had finally arrived: San Francisco. The moment he stepped out of that bus he just burst into tears. Seeing his mother just made him so emotional. Even though he had been there just a couple of seconds, he wanted to go home and rest because a trip like that can exhaust a person so bad.

**The Meeting**

"Let's go out," her sister Rosa said to my mom as they were watching TV. "You just turned eighteen. Let's go dancing."

My mom replied, "Don't be crazy. I have work tomorrow at Pollo Supremo." So, they kept bickering until eventually my mom said yes and they got ready, all dressed up and headed out for an unforgettable night.

*"Salgamos amigo, no tenemos nada más que hacer,"* my dad's friend Omar said to him.

*"Vamos. Pues tengo ganas de salir de todos modo,"* my dad replied.

Rosa and my mom arrived and there was a really long line, but they eventually got inside and just started dancing some *bachata, merengue, cumbia*—every kind of music they loved, they danced to. Little did they know that across that dance floor there stood this guy staring at Rosa and my mom. Then they saw him walk over to Rosa and ask her, *"¿Puedo bailar contigo? Tu y tu hermana son bien bonitas."* Rosa laughed and pushed her younger sister to dance with him. She saw the twinkle Raquel's eye the minute she laid her eyes on him. The night passed, and the hours that they had danced felt like minutes. Milton, this young gentleman, asked her for her name and her number, and she said to him "Maria" and gave him her number. The next day, Milton called "Maria" and asked where she was, and as soon as he found out the address he went over there. At Pollo Supremo, he went in asking for "Maria." Nobody knew a Maria up until he saw my mom coming out from the back and said, "That's her."

Raquel's cheeks turned so red, and she walked up to him and said, "My name isn't Maria. It's actually Raquel." The rest is history. At the age of nineteen, she was pregnant with me. My loving parents, I adore you. You are the light in my world.

**Family**

*These people who I cherish*
*Their kind souls, hearts, and minds*
*There is no way*
*That I'd trade them for anything*
*They have made me into this strong, independent*
*Young woman*
*I am confident, outgoing, and funny*
*All because of them*
*There's no doubt in my mind that they are*
*The reason I am myself*
*I am and forever will be thankful*
*My mom and dad*
*My sisters*
*My tía*
*And my cousins*
*I grew up with them*
*My entire life, they're the only family I know*
*They have never done wrong by me*

*I love you, family*
*Never forget that*
*You guys are my world*

———

**Gennesis G.** *was born in San Francisco and is sixteen years old. Her family are the most loving, caring, and honest people she has in her life. She loves to capture moments through a camera. She enjoys creating. Her favorite time of year is summer. She loves the feeling of summer and the soft touch of sun. She plans on becoming someone successful in life. She wants to be happy.*

# THE HERO JACOB

—

## JACOB G.

There is a house in the forest. Inside the house are three young kids with their grandparents. Sometimes the kids are selfish or maybe mean. The grandparents don't like that they act like that. As the grandparents are relaxing, the kids are being destructive and wrecking the house. The grandparents feel they need to find a way to calm down the kids. The grandpa decides to tell the kids a story about a hero to try and change the way the they act at the house. He tells the kids to all come to the living room so he can start and tell the story...

One hundred years ago, there was a boy named Jacob who lived in a village that was about to be corrupted by the essence called the Great Calamity. The Great Calamity turns you evil if it infects you. The soldiers went off to fight the source of the Great Calamity, but ended up getting wiped out because they didn't work together. Jacob wanted to fight off the Great Calamity, but he wanted to do it differently. He didn't want to go alone like the other soldiers, he wanted to be with others. Jacob told his parents that he wanted to fight, but his parents told him not to because he would be in a life-or-death situation. Jacob told them that he was not going to go straight to the source of the Great Calamity, but instead he was going to go meet up with some other people to help him. His parents were proud of his courage so they ended up letting him go. His dad was a former soldier so he let Jacob use his sword and shield.

Once Jacob was ready, his parents gave their goodbyes and he was off to the Water Domain.

As he is traveling to the Water Domain, he encounters many enemies on the way, but he eventually gets to his destination. When he gets there, he meets the Water Prince, who is swimming in the lake. The Prince tells Jacob he is swimming to get better to become the best in the region. Jacob notices the Prince is wearing a special pair of boots with fins attached to them, letting the Prince swim really fast. Jacob asks the Prince if he could have the boots, but the Prince says only if Jacob beats him in a swimming race and he proves himself worthy.

Jacob and the Prince go to the starting line of the race and start swimming. The Prince is much faster than Jacob mainly because Jacob isn't as experienced a swimmer. The Prince ends up winning and decides to watch Jacob finish the race. The Prince looks at Jacob's face and sees he is trying his best. Once Jacob finishes, the Prince tells Jacob that he sort of cheated because he used the boots.

The Prince tells Jacob to race again, but instead Jacob would use the boots. If Jacob wins he would get to keep the boots. Both Jacob and the Prince go back to the starting line and decide to race again, but instead, Jacob has the boots on. They both race and Jacob is so much faster than before. Both Jacob and the Prince are neck and neck and at the very last stretch, Jacob reaches only slightly ahead and beats the Prince. The Prince tells Jacob that he can keep the boots and to go on in his adventure. Jacob thanks the Prince and leaves soon after.

Jacob thinks about where to go next and he decides to go to the desert to see if he can acquire a hookshot. As he leaves the Water Domain, he sees a giant shrine that is glowing orange. Jacob goes over to it and enters. When he walks in, he is approached by a spider-like figure. It's holding a shield, spear, and a sword and has three legs. Jacob notices that it is guarding a chest locked behind some bars. Jacob wants that chest so he decides to go and attack the spider-like figure. Jacob notices that he can only attack when the sword is out because when he attacks the shield, nothing happens. Two minutes later the figure starts to power up a strong beam, so Jacob starts charging at it with all his might. He ends up destroying it, and the spear, sword, and shield drop. The locked bars also open, revealing the chest behind it. Jacob grabs the sword and shield, but leaves the spear behind. He walks over to the chest and opens it. Inside the chest is a blue tunic and a pair of light brown pants. Jacob takes off his armor and puts on the blue tunic and the pants. He also leaves his old sword and shield to replace them with the sword and shield that he just obtained. Jacob leaves the shrine soon after.

As Jacob is walking to the desert, he gets lost and loses track of where he is, so he decides to climb up a giant mountain to get a good view. As he is walking up, there is purple slime all over the top of the mountain. It is making weird noises. Jacob stops and thinks about what the slime is, and remembers it is what infected all the soldiers that went off to fight the Calamity. Jacob needs to stay away from the slime as he climbs up or he will be infected. As he gets to the top he sees an eye that's sort of popping out of some of the slime—it is constantly opening and closing. Jacob decides to shoot the eye with one of his arrows, and suddenly, all the purple slime disappears. After all the slime disappears, Jacob is free to walk around anywhere on the mountain, so he goes over to the highest ledge of the mountain. To the east, he sees a giant volcano, and to the west, he sees just sand behind some more mountains, so it must be the desert. Jacob now knows where he is located and climbs down the mountain to go to the desert.

Jacob walks for hours and he finally gets to the desert. In the distance, he sees a town, so he decides to walk over to it to see if they have a hookshot. As he gets to the town, there are two tall female guards blocking the entrance. They tell Jacob that this village is only for "foes." Jacob doesn't know what a foe is, so he asks the man sitting just outside the entrance of the village walls. The man tells Jacob that he thinks a foe is female, so only females are allowed in the village. The man also tells Jacob that there are rumors that a man dressed up as a woman and got into the village. Jacob feels stumped and doesn't know what he can do to get inside the village. He decides to walk back and see if he can get a hookshot from the village near the volcano. As he is walking, he notices another village super far out. Jacob walks over to that village and sees a man dressed up as a woman at the top of the building. He climbs up the ladders and talks to him. The man tells him he will give Jacob a pair of his clothes if he pays him 500 rupees. Jacob has 1,322 rupees, so he decides to buy the clothes. Jacob puts the clothes on and walks back over to the first village. He walks through the gates and the tall guards surprisingly don't catch on to him. As he walks around the town, he notices everyone is a female; there is not a single male in sight.

As Jacob walks around, he notices a training area near the entrance of the palace. He walks into the training area and notices there is a hookshot just lying on the table near some guards attacking a dummy. He walks over to the hookshot and brings his hand out to grab it, but one of the guards stops him. The guard then tells Jacob that the hookshot is very uncommon in these kinds of lands. If he wants it he will have to beat her in a one-on-one duel. They both use wooden swords so it won't cause too much injury. Jacob and the guard go to one side of the training area and the other guards go to the other side. The first one to get hit five times loses. They both charge at each other and Jacob immediately gets hit on the right arm and on the side of his body. After Jacob gets hit two times, he decides to walk back a few feet and moves in a circle around the guard. Jacob rushes in and gets two hits on the guard's left and right arm. Jacob then gets hit one more time on his stomach. Jacob gets nervous, and so he toughens up and charges toward the guard. Then once he gets half a foot away, he turns to the guard's right side and gets his final three hits. Jacob is surprised he was able to do that. The guard goes over to the hookshot and gives it to Jacob. He thanks the guard and leaves the town in the desert. Now that he has the hookshot and the boots, he can go over to the castle that was corrupted by the Great Calamity one hundred years ago. Meanwhile, as Jacob is rushing over to the castle, his hometown is on the verge of being corrupted by the Great Calamity.

Before he enters, he changes his clothes back to the blue tunic. As he gets to the entrance, he notices the sky instantly turns purple with black fog surrounding him. He goes in through the side entrance because the main entrance has way too many enemies to fight off. Jacob goes up the castle while trying to stay away from the purple slime. He finally gets to the top floor, but he notices it is just empty. After a few seconds, a giant, dark pile of smoke starts appearing in the middle of the room, so Jacob moves over to the side. Soon after, a giant beast with horns and two swords on each hand appears from the smoke. The beast was known as Calamity Andy. Andy shoots balls of fire at Jacob, so he parries them back with his shield, which stuns Andy. When Andy is parried, Jacob goes and attacks him for a few seconds before he snaps back up. Jacob does it a few times until some of the floor changes to water. As a result, Jacob loses a lot of area to move around on, but if he falls into the water, he could use his special water boots to maneuver quickly around in the water. After a few moments, Jacob notices that Andy is starting to slow down a lot, so Jacob hookshots onto Andy's head and proceeds to kill Andy. Once Andy is defeated, his body turns into smoke and disappears, never be seen again. All the purple slime scattered around the world fades away and everything infected by the Calamity is cured.

The grandpa finished his story about the Hero and the kids also changed the way they acted. The children used to be mean and selfish, but after the story they were not selfish or mean anymore. They learned to act the way that Jacob acted—courageous and brave.

---

*Jacob G. was born in San Francisco. He is fifteen years old. He likes to watch YouTube and play games. He loves cars. Someday in the future, he hopes to have a high-paying job. He is a student at Galileo High School.*

# MY BORDER
—

## ADOLFO H.

In my freshman year of high school, my older brother played football and told me I should try it, so I did. I started every game until one Saturday. It was windy, lots of fog, and I was already at risk with my asthma. It was 8:20 a.m. and the game was at 9:00 a.m. I panicked because if I did well during the game, I would be moved up to varsity. This game, you could say, was very important because I would be able to play with my older brother. The first half had passed and I felt I like I was doing well. In the third quarter, everyone left and right was double-teaming me. I felt pressured because I didn't want to let down my parents. I wanted to make them happy and very proud of me being able to play varsity. Fourth quarter, I rushed the fourth-down blitz, and when I made contact, I felt something snap. I couldn't move my leg, so I started crying because I knew this wasn't good. My teammates carried me out and the nurse told me it felt like I had snapped something. She told my mom I should go get an MRI (x-ray), so we did. Turns out I almost tore my ACL and in order to play I needed a knee brace or surgery.

The doctors told me and my parents it was our choice: I could get a brace or I could get surgery. They said surgery would be the best, but I didn't think so. My parents and I chose not to get surgery. I chose to let it heal and I started thinking what's next, what would I do. I felt very limited in things I could do, so my little brother got me into video games. I started to get distracted and not think about it, and it worked for a little bit. Then I couldn't play with my cousins and have always had the responsibility to take care of my little brother since he is only eleven months younger than me. I always look out for him and always get mad at him, but I try and help him to not make the same mistakes I have made before. My little brother isn't the smartest, but he is very good at video games like *2K* and *Fortnite*. Just like me, he doesn't do the best in school and it is hard to go because he isn't too good at understanding his teachers. Sometimes my mom gives us a break and allows us to show up late to class.

I tried to get my little brother to play football, but as always, he refused. I just thought he wouldn't want to play and maybe he was scared because of what happened to me. My brother and I weren't the greatest friends as we fought every time we played because we would lose or he didn't pass the ball. Playing video games makes me feel distracted and makes me feel like I'm good enough and can do something. When I play with my little brother he makes me feel good and valued. I try being the best at the game or as others call "a tryhard." I do that because it makes my brother feel confident in winning games and not losing, as we both are sore losers.

My border isn't something physical, but it is emotional, as after I got hurt I didn't know what was next or what to do with all of the free time I had after my injury. I tried to distract myself with video games like *2K* and *Fortnite*. So far, I have felt withdrawn and don't feel the same. It's like I feel like I can't talk to anybody and can't trust anybody. I have tried to think of ways to get around this border and things I can do instead of football. So far, all I have thought of is video games.

This didn't only affect me, but I feel like it affected my family because they are used to seeing us play sports and being out on the field making them cheer. I had thought that if I worked out, it could give me the strength and confidence I need to start getting new things to do. I think if I do that it could help, but the only problem is I'm not motivated because I gave up on sports and thought it was over. Recently it got a little harder since about three months ago, I got a girlfriend. She goes to this school and has asked me to open up to her, but I said I couldn't. She always asks if I want to talk about it, but I try and change the subject because I don't really trust anybody. The reason for this is when I got my injury I felt like I let my family down and I wouldn't be able to make them happy. I felt useless and like I wasn't good enough, so I ruined my relationship and now my girlfriend doesn't trust me as she would've if I hadn't messed around.

––––––––

*Adolfo H. was born in Pittsburg, California. He is fifteen years old and likes to play football and different sports. He wants to become a football player. He also likes to play video games and* Fortnite. *His favorite food is pizza.*

# MY FRIEND JORB

—

**KEVIN H.**

The year was 2017. I was at home talking to my friend Rey over the computer about a few games that we should buy and play together. The air was cold and it felt like I was living in Antarctica. I could smell the vanilla shampoo that my mother uses. It's like I was attracted to it. I felt like a honeybee that wanted some of the sweet nectar that flowers provided. A fresh cup of coffee was sitting on my desk along with the bowl of rice that I had prepared for breakfast. It was around ten in the morning and I usually don't wake up that early on weekends, but I went to sleep earlier the night before. After chatting with Rey for a couple of minutes, he asked if it would be okay for me to meet his new friend that he had met over an online game.

After a decent amount of time, Rey convinced me to at least introduce myself to his friend. We shall call his friend "Jorb" since it was what I called him to remember his real name. The idea of talking to a person I didn't know was very hard for me. It's always tough for me to meet new people and talk with them since I'm very socially awkward. When I do, I start to panic and think about ruining my first impression for a person I've never met before. A few minutes passed by, and Jorb joined the call along with Rey and they instantly started talking to each other.

As Jorb was talking, I assumed that he was white based on the pitch and tone of his voice. Being the curious little fourteen-year-old I was at the time, I texted Rey privately and asked him what race Jorb was. He responded and told me to ask him myself since I was so curious. So, I did. It turns out Jorb was actually African American and was adopted by a family in Philadelphia. He talked about how he was born in Philadelphia and his family adopted him along with his other siblings that weren't related to each other at all. I had never really met anyone who was adopted before, let alone become friends with them. It was hard for me to understand that Jorb was adopted and I wasn't sure how to react to that.

"I had never really met anyone who was adopted before, let alone become friends with them. It was hard for me to understand that Jorb was adopted and I wasn't sure on how to react to that."

It was difficult to cross the border and become friends with Jorb. Uncertainty fell over me as I wasn't sure how to act around him. As Rey and Jorb continued their conversation, silence set in since there wasn't much to talk about between the three of us. The silence was so quiet that it felt like I was in a ghost town. It wasn't like I had been talking that much anyways since it was hard for me to butt into the conversation between the two of them. I started thinking about being adopted and having biological parents that I didn't know. In the end, it didn't really matter to me anymore. I started talking to Jorb a lot more over the course of a few days, and we got into deep conversations about our lives. We talked about our fears and careers that we are trying to aim for in our futures.

After talking for a year and a half now, I've learned so much about Jorb and his family. I could go on and on about him now. His favorite color is blue, he has siblings that are adopted as well. He plays the same video games, and his clothing choices match what I wear on a daily basis. The most important thing that I learned about him was his personality. He's funny and has those random moments where he's just a clown. The border between me and Jorb wasn't really a racial issue, it was about having thoughts about what Jorb's life was like being adopted. It was hard to overcome, and it took some courage and understanding to know more about Jorb. By now, Jorb and I get along pretty well, and I have even met a few of his friends over time.

---

*Kevin H. was born in San Francisco. He is fifteen years old. He enjoys talking to friends and playing basketball. A life goal he has is to become a game designer or concept artist.*

# ANTICIPATION

—

## STEVE H.

This story begins on San Bruno in San Francisco. I was with friends and my cousin, attending a small video game tournament at the Microsoft store. We took the bus to get downtown. First, we met up at Walgreens around 2:00 p.m. on San Bruno. I was one of the first ones there on time, besides my cousin, Phu. Despite us being cousins, we look really different from each other. I'm skinny and he is more muscular than I am. My hair looks like what my friends describe as a bowl cut, and Phu has a Korean K-pop star haircut. He is more neatly dressed with jeans and a black shirt, while I often wear black sweatpants and a navy-blue fur jacket. When a conversation gets going, I'm usually the one mostly talking, while Phu doesn't really speak much. Phu was on another team with a different group of friends.

We stood around on our phones waiting for everyone else to get there. I wasn't good at starting conversation, so it was a few moments of awkward silence. I kept looking at my phone to look at the time, getting annoyed at the fact that my friends were late again, but to be fair they were always late.

After what felt like a long time, from a distance I saw someone running toward us. It was my friend Tommy, who finally arrived where we were supposed to meet. Tommy is best described among our friends as a walking skeleton, short, with messy hair because he never washes it in the morning, and you can tell it is him from a distance from his signature gray fur jacket. He is better at conversation, and he began talking to us, breaking the ice in our little group. He asked, "Where are the rest of the losers?"

"Probably still at home," I replied.

"So, who is playing what role?" he asked.

"I'm going to play support. Justin is playing Jungler. Gloria is Mid Lane. Jonathan is Top Lane and Brian is ADC (Attack Damage Carry)," I answered.

The game takes place on a map called "Summoner's Rift." Both halves of the map are mirrored from each other and form a funnel shape. It has three lanes where the two teams fight, which are defended by three destructible defense towers, each being separated by the jungle, which has monsters in it. Two rivers connect the top and both side lanes to the mid lane. The lanes lead up to each team's base where the Nexus is, which you need to defend or you lose.

The other team will probably check our match histories and profiles to see and ban the champions that we're best at. So, if they ban Justin's Kayn, Jonathan and Justin will switch places. As a support, my job is to protect and help Brian, the ADC, get kills, and stay alive. Brian, as the ADC, is a marksman who deals consistent damage to the enemy, and is overall vulnerable to enemy attacks because of their low health and armor. Top Lane, which is controlled by Jonathan, has the tanks of the team in charge of starting team fights. Mid Lane, who is Gloria, is the assassin of our team who tries to quickly kill the enemy ADC or people with low health in general. They deal high amounts of damage, but are also squishy with low HP (health points). And finally, the Jungler is not in the lane, but in the jungle, killing the monster camps to get gold and experience. They're in charge of securing team buffs like dragons, Herald, Rift Scuttler, and Baron Nashor. The Jungler often comes to other lanes to kill the enemy laner and put the ally laner ahead.

We talked about what roles we would be playing at the tournament as we waited for everyone else to arrive. We spoke about random stuff that I don't even remember until the rest came together. They were Jimmy,

Jonathan, and Brian. They were different from each other in physical looks and personality, but shared the same hobbies and interests. We met each other through mutual friends and became friends because of our shared interests and humor. Now, being late by minutes, we waited for the 8 bus.

The bus arrived and we got on. As we were on the bus, we spoke to each other to pass the time. Thirty minutes passed and we saw our stop getting closer.

"We're at our stop," Gilbert informed us. The bus driver jolted, putting a stop to the mechanical serpent. As it stopped, it let out a dying hiss and its power-driven doors opened up. Gilbert was the first one to get off, and we followed behind. We stood at the bus stop downtown. It was on a red brick sidewalk surrounded by tall office buildings with its walls nearly covered by windows. Tons of people walked across the wide streets.

We began walking toward the Westfield Mall, passing by buildings. Finally, we arrived at the Westfield Mall. This was the first time my friends and I, besides Brian, saw Gloria in person. We met her online when my friend Brian invited her into our party in League and Discord. She was extremely toxic in League. When we saw her, she was short and had brown hair, completely different from how I had imagined her. We sat down at the computers and waited one hour at the Microsoft store for them to get it set up and ready for the tournament to start.

It finally hit three o'clock, and it was time for the tournament to begin. We had already entered our team names and members before it started. Four different teams were next to us as we waited. Tension was building to see which teams would be fighting next. A man in a cerulean blue collared shirt took a step toward us. Judging from the employee uniform, I knew he was the host. Then he spoke up, "Sorry, the laptops are still updating the game. We're going to have to wait for it to finish."

I felt a little disappointed, like a child waiting for his mother to finish talking to her friend at a grocery store, but by now I'd already waited a week, so I was willing to wait a little longer. My friend Tommy and I played around with the paint software on the small tablets in the store and drew *League of Legends* characters to pass the time waiting. We took turns choosing who to draw. Tommy chose first. He chose a nightmarish, vicious, enormous purple monster from the Void that can devour anything with a whole row of sharp teeth and two horns at the sides of its head curling toward the front. Its name was Cho'Goth. In a 2D way, I began drawing the mouth of the beast. I drew a trapezoid-shaped mouth with a triangular set of fangs, three on top and three on the bottom of the mouth. Then I drew a rectangle head with decently drawn curved horns. My next obstacle was creating the eyes, so I drew them in an oval shape, with one on each side of the face.

Feeling proud of my drawing, I announced to my friend that I was finished with my creation. He told me to wait a little longer as he finished up the final touches of his artwork. Mildly annoyed, I looked back to my tablet and just doodled. Finally, he stated he was finished. We started comparing our work and I looked at his. I was able to determine mine was distinctively superior. Tommy and I kept illustrating for a while, until we heard a voice announce, "Everyone, we're beginning the tournament." We both looked around to see who was talking and saw it was the host. I walked up with my team to see who was going to be up.

"The team who wins will stay on and fight the next team," informed the host.

Knowing that whoever went up first had no chance of winning the tournament because of the fact that they'd have to win every single game made me anxious at the chance of my team going up.

"Team Something versus Team Woah," he told us.

I was relieved that it wasn't us going up this time. I sat down on a side bench next to the gaming laptops where everyone played. We sat there and watched them play as forty minutes passed by. Team Something destroyed the enemy's Nexus, winning the game. The ones in Team Woah got off the seats and walked out of the room. Before the host could inform us which team was going up next, an eager team quickly sat down at the laptop tables and got ready. The ones who just barged in were Team Thing. The host, seeming unconcerned about it, sat down and watched. After getting their voice communication and accounts logged in, they invited each other into a custom game. Once everyone joined the lobby, they started the game.

Tired of waiting, I turned to Brian and asked, "Do you want to buy something to eat as we wait?"

"What are we going to buy anyways?" he questioned. I paused and began to think.

"How about the frozen yogurt place around the corner?" I answered.

"Who else is going with us?" Brian asked.

"I don't know. Ask them," I said while turning my head toward the rest of my team.

Brian went to them and asked if they wanted to buy frozen yogurt with us. Jonathan, Tommy, and Justin wanted to come along, but Jimmy and Gloria didn't want to buy frozen yogurt and stayed to watch the game.

Tommy led the group toward the yogurt place. We got to the store and it was colorful with smooth yellow-colored walls and wooden floors. They had yogurt dispensers of different flavors along the walls. I grabbed a lime green paper yogurt cup and walked toward the vanilla dispenser. I pulled down the smooth white plastic lever and the vanilla slowly descended into the cup. I moved my cup in a circular motion to get the most yogurt that I could. I let go of the lever and decided to get some toppings. I went to the trays with different toppings like strawberries and chocolate bits. I picked up a clear plastic claw grabby thingy and got some strawberries for my yogurt. Done, I went to the cashier and handed her my yogurt cup. She put it on a gray metal scale to determine the price.

She looked up and told me, "That'll be $5.47." I handed her six dollars.

"Thank you, come again," the cashier said as a goodbye.

I took my change and yogurt and left the store. Joe, Nathan, and Tom were already done and waiting for the rest of us. Tommy took a glance at what I got.

"Yours is so plain. You've got to add different flavors to it and more toppings like mine." He showed me his yogurt cup and it had two different colors of yogurt. One greenish and one white. I'm guessing one of them was vanilla. He added a bunch of fruits and some gummy bears.

I took a spoonful of my yogurt and realized the flavor I had wasn't vanilla. It was some kind of weird sour-ish flavor that my aunt used to give me as a kid.

"Dude, I got the wrong flavor," I told Jonathan.

"Ha, nice job," he mocked. Brian and Justin were done and everyone began walking back to the tournament.

We sat down on the benches and watched the game as it went on. Twenty minutes went by and Team Something won. Then another team went on to play and we had to wait forty minutes for them to finish. As the tournament went on, we never got to play. We waited and waited for hours. It was already eight o'clock and I was tired of waiting and wanted to play. It was down to the last two teams. Our team, Team Not Good, and Team CYC. Team CYC was made up of friends and mutual friends: William the platinum-ranked ADC, Aiden the gold-ranked support, Chris the bronze player Jungler, some dude I don't know as the gold player Mid Lane, and Brandon, a silver player Top Lane. We were cautious of William; he was the highest-ranked player on the team and had a concerningly large champion pool to pick from. So, banning him wasn't possible, as he would just pick a different champion to play as. Our plan was to ban their Mid Lane Zed, who we saw destroy the enemy team last game. For the rest, we did not know who to ban. So, we would just ban our counter picks. Team CYC knew all of our best champions, because my friend Desmond told them. Like what the hell, man?

I was nervous for the lane, but I was willing to play against them. Gloria was very nervous and kept saying, "Let's just give up and go home."

I told her, "We just waited so long. I'm not just going to give up and go home." I was unsure about how everyone else felt about this. We went toward the laptops and sat down on the peach-colored stools with wooden, black-cushioned seats. I began setting up everything: voice communication, and logging my account into League. I clicked the

Discord icon with the white game controller enclosed in a purple square. Discord opened up and I pressed my fingers onto the laptop keyboard to log in. An anti-bot identify check popped up onto my screen. I had to keep clicking on which picture had a car in it. I kept clicking and clicking away at those damn boxes. I did it so many times, it was starting to feel like a cookie clicker game. After around five minutes, I finally logged into my Discord. Shortly after I finished, everyone else that had the same problem finished confirming their identity. I joined the voice communication with my team.

I opened up League and logged in quickly. A voice spoke up and asked, "Who is going to make the private game?"

"I'll make the game, send me a friend request. My account name is Chris123," Chris replied.

Justin sent the friend request to Chris and joined his lobby. Shortly after, Justin invited the rest of us to the game. Then the game started.

The champion declaration screen went up, I selected Blitzcrank, a yellow robot whose signature move is launching its right arm out toward the enemy, grabbing and pulling the person toward him.

---

***Steve H.*** *was born in San Francisco. He's currently sixteen years old. Steve's hobby is to play video games, like* League of Legends *for example. He is unsure of what he wishes to be in the future as his career path.*

# SIX POEMS IN SEARCH OF MY BORDER

—

**JASMINE J.**

**Beginning**
It's not fair that people who I care a lot for
are on the other side of that border I don't
Show any affection, no emotion sometimes
Because in reality I'm so sad and depressed
Inside, but sometimes I have to suck it up.

**Papa**
*Un hombre* who is *Loco,* who loves his kids
Makes jokes and makes me laugh. A hard
Working dad with two jobs and proud to be
From Mexico and deserves much more.

**El Grito de México**
A day out of the year that here in the U.S.
in Civic Center, Mexicans celebrate *El Grito de
México* to remind them of Mexico. There
is food, mariachi so loud that makes
You want to dance. Music colors red
white and green that define the flag
and at eight o'clock exactly everything stops
And All together we yell *Que Viva México!*
A day to Remember what it feels like to be in
Mexico.

**Mama**
A mother who loves and cares for her children
Who has a beautiful Dominican accent and wants
The best for her family. She has been through hell
And back, but got through it *una mamá con un
Corazón Grande.*

**Sancocho**
*Una sopa hecho en Santo Domingo que es
Sabrosa.* This meal makes me feel like I'm in the
Dominican Republic every single time I eat it.
If you have a headache *comete un sancocho*
If your stomach hurts, eat some *sancocho,* this
Meal helps you warm up and feel good. It's the
Best medicine.

### Living in Two Worlds

I'm from the United States, but I'm living in two
Worlds: my mother's culture, my dad's culture.
And those cultures are a part of me and proud
To be a Latina, I will never be ashamed of who
I am or where my parents came from. Because
Being a Latina I should not have to impress any
White person for them to see that we're all
Equal. I will never let anyone's racism be a
Border between me and my future.

---

*Jasmine J. is sixteen years old. She is half Mexican and half Dominican and she likes to listen to a lot of music and she likes to dance. She is a sophomore in high school and likes drawing and studying photography.*

# WRINKLY HERBS

—

## TRACY K.

My grandma loves talking to strangers on the bus, and sometimes she will just jump into any conversation she hears.

"Hey, where are you going?" my grandma asked the lady in the blue windbreaker jacket on the bus.

"I gotta go buy groceries," the kind lady replied back.

"I need to go to North East Medical Services for her doctor's appointment," she said, while pointing at me.

There's not a single time she doesn't find someone she knows on the bus or in the streets. Then, there is me who has no friends. She is always louder than a fire truck. She can sound like she is arguing on the phone instead of having a normal conversation. We can never stay together for too long because she talks too much and makes me feel embarrassed. That would be my time to put my earbuds on and play music on full blast.

Me and my grandma get closer and closer every day. I've been following her since I have arrived in this world, but we have so many differences, like our everyday lives, for example. I notice them especially when I'm with her on the bus to Chinatown.

She is not just a regular grandma who carries a cane around. She loves to look young and dress up, and I'm the opposite. She would also agree with me about that (especially wedding dates when I have to wear

56

dresses, which I hate the most). She dyes her hair like every teenager or adult, usually in the color of burgundy like a plum or dark purple like an eggplant. I'm proud when I'm the one who helps my family members dye their hair. It is very fun, but the strong smell of the dye always kills me.

"Your hair has to look nice, even if your outfit is ugly," she said while combing her hair, and I laughed in the corner of my room.

The first thing I hate in Chinatown is the smell of the herbs.

"They taste bitter and they smell so bitter. Sometimes they can smell sweet or minty, but I don't like them overall," I said.

"Well you need to go in and help me buy them. I'm busy, I need to go pick up your sister," she said while she walked away.

I don't know anything about Chinese herbs, and the worst thing is that I have a bad memory, so I forgot which ones she told me to buy. All I know is that they don't smell good. My Chinese is not as good as everyone thinks because I never learned how to read it until high school. I don't get how people eat this. She gets mad at me for buying the wrong ones or buying the bad looking ones. The point is, they all look the same to me. The herbs are either in the color of brown or red and they are always dried so they are always wrinkly.

"Which ones do you need me to buy again?" I asked on the phone, one minute after she left.

"The red dates, they're round and they're red," she said in every way to make me understand.

When she came back I could already tell she was mad, "It's not this one," she said, but in a tone that told me she was already done with me.

"Well, it's not my fault, I don't know my Chinese characters," I replied calmly.

She pointed out the ones I should have bought, but they just looked exactly the same. She kept the kind I bought anyways. It was probably something useful. I only remember the ones that she cooks with regularly and the ones she puts in her herb soups.

I just left her and went to buy my own supplies, including my favorite drink, bubble milk tea. It's something I thought my grandma wouldn't enjoy, but actually she likes to drink it. (Except the boba because she thinks it's really bad for you. Some say it's made from rubber.)

There are always times when she objects and says, "Don't drink too much; it's too sweet."

"Not like I drink it every day," I reply.

"Still, it cost too much and it is unhealthy for your body," she explains.

I still go anyway without her knowing. She is always mad whenever I get home late and start my homework late and she explains that I'm wasting too much electricity and continues, saying how we use too much regularly and the bills get higher and higher. The days that I'm not home either I'm at school, or I'm actually hanging out with my friends at the mall or in the movies or at dinner.

My grandma gets angry at everything, even the smallest things. A moment that she got kind of mad was when my grandpa was in a car accident, but it was only a small scratch to the car.

"Your grandpa could have honked at that car. They apparently don't even know how to drive!" she screamed at us for the fourteenth time.

That is when I got annoyed, "Can you be quiet? You have said that so many times, I can repeat everything back to you word for word," I said in frustration.

"It's not like you can go back in time," I continued, but I did wish this could happen though. Then she went back to what she was doing before.

After that incident, there was another small mistake that angered her again. It was one night when I experienced something that I thought would never happen. The school year was about to end and my friend's birthday was on June 4, so I asked my friend if she wanted to go celebrate with other friends at a Korean BBQ restaurant. During the time we were there, I was so annoyed with my phone.

"When are you coming home?" my grandma asked on the phone.

"Almost," I replied back and ended the phone call.

Five minutes later.

"When are you going to leave?" she asked back, but louder this time.

"Not yet," I replied again.

I had already told her that I was going to come home late and I also called my grandpa to come pick me up. No one lived near me at that time so I was still afraid to go home myself, especially when I was far away. That day, my grandma called and asked us to go buy sugar for her coffee. She would rather drink instant coffee than actually boiling it. We headed to Safeway near our house and ran through the aisle. We didn't know which one to buy, all we knew was that the packaging was light blue, but there were still lots of options. We quickly grabbed a box and left. Safeway was going to close any second since it was very late. I was very tired so I took a very short nap in the smooth car ride, but it could be bumpy along the way. When we got home, we gave the box of sugar to my grandma.

"This is not the one I use usually," she said.

"There was so much and we don't even know which one you use," my grandpa replied.

"Go return it and get me the one I use," she said, annoyed.

"I am not going back. If you don't want to use it, then throw it away!" my grandpa yelled, so she threw the newly bought box of sugar in the garbage.

That was the first time he went to buy the sugar—usually she asks my mom instead. Sometimes my grandma will just take a few packets of sugar home from Starbucks. My grandma needs to drink at least one cup of coffee a day just to stay energized and awake. When she got so angry and she threw the packets of sugar away, it was surprising and all I could do was watch because that was the first time she got so angry just from the wrong packs of sugar. I thought they would throw more stuff around, but nope, they didn't. It was a weekend, so I didn't need to go to sleep that early, but if I had I would have told her to stop shouting because of school the next day. My mom would probably have experienced when my grandma got angry before, but that was literally my first time and for something pretty small. My younger sister was not listening, she was just going on her laptop and watching her YouTube videos. After their argument on sugar they got back to normal with just my grandpa finishing his dinner.

It didn't take long for her to calm back down and become fine again. I thought that she would still be mad and continue her argument, but even my grandpa had stopped. After arguments, you can hear her just whispering to herself. Even though they are whispers, her whispers are very loud. Usually I would be telling her to just let it go. When she continues to talk, I always just ignore her, but sometimes my grandma would be correct. This time was only about a pack of sugar, so I didn't have a side and I didn't want to be part of any arguments. Choosing sides is not my thing and neither is arguing with people, but my grandma can just make up things to argue for, especially about me.

My grandma gets really mad, especially when it's about her siblings and her mother. Recently her brother left their mom to pay for her own taxi fee instead of paying for it. My grandma was angry and had said she would need to call him and yell at him. I thought that her brother should be the one paying also since her mother is very old and she was the one who needs the money to spend. I would also be angry and I thought he should be more responsible since their mother is elderly. I felt that my grandma and I are not so different from each other.

I can understand how my grandma felt when she was shouting at her own siblings. I always shout at my own sibling, too, when she does something wrong. Being the oldest of your siblings you would have lots of responsibility. When I was asked to take care of my sibling, I would make sure she ate and finished her homework.

I used to have many stuffed animals, but my grandma would always say that they collect too much dust. I am still into characters, but I only like one kind, the BT21 characters. My grandma and parents don't have a problem with me collecting the dolls and keychains, but still I think I should keep the amount I should get at a minimum. They can be really expensive so I really don't want to waste any more money on things that may not be useful.

At home we still listen to all my grandma's childhood stories, like how when she was younger she used to stalk lovers and watch them in the trees. I love telling stories of my life to my friends, too, or usually I would tell my friends what my grandma told me. My friend is not really smart, so she tends to copy many things like homework or school work, but I usually tell her that she shouldn't copy everything and if she doesn't pass this class she can just fail and have to take this class again. I get very serious when it comes to school just because I don't want to fail myself and because I also don't want my friends to fail their classes either. Seeing how I used to act in middle school and how I act now is so different. In middle school I rarely did homework or I never finished it. Seeing how I've become more mature is surprising, but sometimes I still don't understand how to choose my herbs.

––––––––––

*Tracy K. was born in San Francisco and is fifteen years old. She loves to dance and perform for audiences. Her favorite place to visit would be China. Her goal is to finish high school and get a scholarship to UCLA.*

# SUNNY SMILES

—

## SERGIO M.

**Prologue**

Born and raised in San Francisco, California, I've always grown up preferring to be alone over being in big crowds. I like doing my own thing. I've found that when I take a step back from others, it helps me be more creative. I've learned to let out emotion through many forms of art, whether it's graphic design, drawing, writing, or photography. Even my style and the way I dress is a form of art I let out. I've always found beauty and heartbreak in everything I lay my eyes on.

"Sunny Smiles" was motivated by the simple fact of always being alone. I notice that loneliness isn't something that only I go through. There isn't always someone or something to shed your tears on. At times, all you really have is yourself. This poem was written and inspired by the frown that I constantly cover behind a smile. The single line in Spanish is a small tribute toward my ethnicity. Spanish is my first language.

Everyone has a place in their heart and spine where darkness and grief quietly lie. Just because agony isn't shown or appreciated doesn't mean that this place of pain doesn't exist. My meaning in the words written in this poem go toward being able to overcome pain and heartache, no matter how long it takes or what has to be done to do so. Every day is a new day with a new opportunity to shine. Pain is a form of reality just as much as happiness is. The sun always shines to see another day; the sun always overcomes the gray clouds that make everything gloomy. At times, being on your own turns into something that you want to run away from. You want someone. Sometimes you want to let the border down and other times you want to avoid people and isolate yourself.

Being lonely when I just want to isolate myself from others' comes naturally when I'm with a group that doesn't spark any activity in my head. I'd prefer to go away on my own rather than being the odd one out in a group. At family gatherings, I can be sitting alone, feeling everything but warmth from everyone else. I'm not in a bad mood or anything, but I just get in my thoughts. People invite me out. They aren't my crowd; if I showed my face or made an appearance, I'd end up finding reasons to get away. I remember I was at a birthday party one time, and I wasn't really feeling the vibe, so I just cut a corner and left. I do that—leave to be by myself—frequently when I'm with different people. It's funny because I feel alone, but then I want to be alone.

When I first wrote this, I put thought into it, but there really wasn't much consideration to what I was writing. And then I kept reading and reading it over again. I wrote this poem in the beginning of the year, and then I started adding more topics like heartbreak and going through painful emotions. It felt like I accomplished something, nothing big, but on that day, I felt happiness in telling myself I wrote something today. My roof…it's very small. It's just a step that I sit on, a very narrow space that's gated off. There are plants there. There's gravel covering the roof. There's always a dog that's barking out of the window. I can see trees in the distance from big parks. I can see the side of the city that most people don't see. The sun always comes up and down at the peak. When I go there at night, it's the same thing, but I stare at the moon and the stars. That is where I wrote this poem, where I took a simple page in my notebook to make something new. I've never written my own poetry before. This poem is meant to have its own interpretation for every reader who lays eyes on these words, for everyone having their own challenges in life, for everything that seems difficult in this exact moment. It'll all be okay.

**Sunny Smiles**

Days are sunny
Smiles are showing
The sun is out, but the words written are done in the dark
The smiles are out, but the faces showing them all fall apart
Days are sunny
Smiles are showing
Gray clouds make the sun disappear
Smiles turn upside down from the inside out
Days are sunny
Smiles are showing
The sun is glowing
Smiles are pouring
Days are sunny
Smiles are showing
The sun is gone, smiles are snoring
The earth is turning, smiles are hurting
A painful truth slowly showing…
Days turn dark
Smiles are gone
The fact that you're alone
With a heart that's never curing
In an endless whirl that keeps on twirling
Along with a life that just keeps on going
Tripping with heart and soul just to get away
Finding a smile, hoping it stays
We all face demons
And we all face angels
Each lying on a shoulder
Hoping for a heart, yet still in danger
A raging mess that can't be stable
Behind a broken heart that strikes as painful

Lies a beautiful face that strikes as faithful

A gorgeous rose that comes to blossom

Is the reflection in the mirror far across from boredom

A smile in that rain? Yes I know I saw some

Everyone smiles, yet darkness is the outcome

*Enamorado de tu sonrisa pero los demonios golpean tus ojos*

I can't make a smile out of my face below those

No matter where the soul goes

I'm afraid

But my happiness is something I can't betray

In love with love, but nowadays it's all foul play

That doesn't matter, tomorrow is a new day

Everything is okay

Let the days be gray

Let the smiles pour

Everything is okay

I'll fix up to see the sun another day

Once more

———————

**Sergio M.** *was born in San Francisco, California and is sixteen years old. He grew up in a Spanish-speaking household with a mom "Ma," dad "Pa," brother "Kia," and sister "Mona." He loves to make art and loves to have a psychedelic mindset when it comes to making imagery out of any art form. He loves to be abstract. His goal is to make any art that comes to mind and get acknowledged for it. He dreams to one day be the best father ever, and plans to keep ambition close.*

# FEAR

—

## JULIAN M.

I woke up in the hospital confused, wondering where I was. Seeing my parents sitting on the chairs, waiting for something to happen. My vision cleared, and I tried to stand up, but found myself held back. I felt like I'd been tied down. I heard my parents say, "NO!"

Fear is a border; it manipulates us to change our actions and how we feel. It's a perceptible border inside us. A tangible border that obstructs my livelihood. Physically, this border was temporary. However, mentally this border is permanent, like a scar engraved onto my brain.

"You can't stand up." I started giggling as I kept trying to stand up from the hospital bed. Once I gave up and settled down, I started asking questions. "What the heck happened?" I was hit by a car, my parents explained. I could feel the IV going through my veins. I was in shock. Confused, I asked, "How come it wasn't my older brother, Eduardito (who happens to be prone to accidents)? It's just weird that it happened to me."

I don't remember what happened, but people told me different details of the accident. From what I put together, I was asked to go to Safeway with my friend, and I accepted. We left the school and started walking. We crossed a long street where cars pass through a lot, which has no stoplights. We went into Safeway, got our items, and then, on our way back, crossing the same long street…BAM! We got hit by a car and went flying across the street, from one sidewalk to the other. I was hit by an elementary school teacher who was drunk at 8:00 a.m. Soon after, I was rushed to the hospital.

Then the pain started to kick in. My left leg was a broken twig. My head felt like a million daggers. I was covered in scabs. Even my bone was scarred. I had to stay in the hospital for months, trapped in boredom and pain. Not allowed to get up, I couldn't even use the bathroom because of some pills that held back my waste for days. Conversing was my only entertainment. Different family came to visit throughout the day.

Months later, I'm leaving the hospital in a wheelchair being taken to the car. Eventually, I lost the wheelchair, I lost the crutches, but one thing that didn't want to leave is of course my memories, my mental state. Still, to this day when I see a car through my peripheral vision, I flinch. That is of course because of the fear that has been tattooed into brain, a new sense of danger.

I'm not the only person with tattoos of fear; many have been given to people, which later grow into a border that collapses on you, taking control of your body. Just like a tattoo is a visual expression of something that starts off in your head or your heart, fear also begins inside, and, depending how you deal with it, can become outwardly visible. Taking the wrong path makes the tattoo ink flow through your veins, little by little turning your heart black. Making you take certain moves you don't want. Changing your opinions. Taking control over your love, but don't be afraid.

––––––

*Julian M. was born in San Francisco, California. He has four sisters and two brothers. He loves to play games (board games, video games, etc.). His favorite weather is rainy.*

# ON THE MOVE
—

## FLORANTE M.

Why am I walking into class when there are fifteen minutes left? Oh wait. That's right. I was at the wrong station, lost and confused. I was late yesterday and on Monday, and hopefully I can get this right by tomorrow. I hate being forced to move from one home to another, especially this last move. I hate living in this almost desolate suburb across the bay, and far from the heavily populated city. The world is unfamiliar to me and my new experiences frighten me. But this all happened because of *him*.

He always seemed like the perfect person, someone to look up to, and a role model, until the day he changed. We were tied together once, but as time passed we began to rip farther and farther away from each other, until we were opposites like fire and ice, never to agree with each other. I never understood the things he did or who he did them for, but I definitely knew it was building a border between a father and a son. Having his name makes me wish that I was at the top of Twin Peaks, yelling out loud and releasing the burden. I look at my reflection, seeing his face on mine, and I feel heavy rain clouds floating over my head, forever pouring down on me until I am soaking wet. He does not make a living, he does not contribute to anything, and he does not care about anyone but himself. The worst thing he did was nothing, while the rest of us were struggling to live. In this city, no one can survive alone and no can give up, but he became useless when he did. I had no money, no life, no safety, so why not run away?

Today is moving day. I carried the boxes in and out of the home that I will never see again, like a dream that disappears when you wake up. The white block-shaped house with wide windows facing the streets and stairs leading up to a dark wooden door stuck on the steepest hill was being wiped away from my memory. I had grabbed lunch one last time from the restaurant down the street where the aroma of sizzling meats spreads around the neighborhood, and I said goodbye to the view from the top of the hill of the shining skyscrapers standing over the people downtown.

As I walk into my new home, I open the door and only a little sunlight lights up the low-ceilinged room. When the sky is dark, the room's source of light is the little dull lamp sitting beside my bed. Every night, I wake up to voices from another family living in the home through the thin white door in the corner of the room. The bills made it so that soon enough it was time to move out again—unfortunately out of the city this time.

I do not have the pleasure to roam around my new, dull town because the buses rarely pass and are many steps away from my home. Throughout the day, I hear the sounds of cars raging at each other on the highway, and motorcycles rumbling through my window. My neighborhood seems perfect until a package arrives at my door and randomly disappears. The sound of random shots and dark explosions spreading throughout the night are muffled by the midnight train. Well, I am glad that I am away from *him* and comfortably living in an affordable community.

Today, the train window perfectly displays the construction sites forming around the bay, with industries that will soon rise up from the ground, and little homes stacked together like books in a library. I arrive at Market Street, feeling as cold as a never-ending snowstorm, and hop on the bus passing through the rushing herd of extravagant executives downtown to the produce markets of Chinatown. On this morning, I am feeling exhausted from the journey to school, when the sky is dark and the smell of morning mist fills the air. I finally arrive home late in the evening when the rushing city quietly sleeps.

Nights on the train are like walking through a pitch-black cemetery alone. Looking out the window, the night is dark and misty and the lights are low on the train with only a few passengers seated. One time, I was targeted by a man who was trying to trick me and steal my phone. Another time, there was someone who pushed me to try and reach into my pocket and snatch some cash. I usually end up stepping onto the wrong train and falling asleep, finding myself miles away from home.

One year later and my challenges, struggles, confusion, and anxiety washed away like a wave slowly making its way back into the sea after it has wrecked a ship. The differences helped me realize that once in a while hardship stabs you in the back, but the wounds embedded in your heart and mind will heal if you are patient. Thinking about my journey in life locks me down in my bed, but I find the energy to rise up because I have friends and family who light me up.

———

*Florante M.* *was born in the Philippines. He grew up in San Francisco. He is fifteen years old. He likes photography and to be outdoors. He is curious about new things and will one day start an adventure around the world. Writing has helped him express his inner feelings about life.*

# HOW CHANGING THE CITY CHANGED ME
—

**ADRIEL N.**

G entrification. **It happens** everywhere but not everyone sees it. Before I joined Youth Organizing Home and Neighborhood Action (YOHANA), I was blind. I was blind to the fact that our city is getting gentrified and residents like me don't even see it. When I joined YOHANA, my eyes were opened to the real world. I saw the problems that are occurring in the community, in *our* community: police brutality, racism, homelessness, oppression, gentrification, and the system itself that puts us down. These problems must be solved and there are people who put their hearts on the table so that they can be.

Here's where everything started. It was the last week of school and I was on the bus with my friend on our way home.

I told him, "I hope I get accepted in this garden project job during the summer."

He replied, "I mean, you could just join this internship with me. It's really fun."

I wanted to join the garden project job because it paid more. Also, I had a couple of friends doing it and they all said it was easy. It wasn't easy trying to decide whether I should try to apply for the garden project or the internship, but later that day, I received an email from someone in the garden project program. He said that they had accepted all the applicants and I didn't get in. So, after some thinking, I made a decision and I texted my friend about taking the internship.

He said, "Cool! I will give you the application for the internship tomorrow."

That was one of the best decisions I ever made. It changed my life. I used to be this guy who went straight home after school, this guy who was lazy, not a part of any programs, did homework then played video games all night. But when I became part of this group, I found out that I could be part of something else, something bigger.

After about two weeks of the Land is Life internship (an internship that is funded by the San Francisco Public Utilities Commission that teaches kids about environmental racism within the context of the SOMA neighborhood), some of the people there invited me to this group called YOHANA. I was very unsure if I should join this group because they said that they usually have meetings on Saturdays at 6:00 p.m. and the meetings usually take two hours. I wasn't sure if my mom would let me get home that late, so I had to talk to her and explain that I was doing something not just for myself, but also for the community. My mom had suspicions about this organization because I told her about the things we do and she didn't like the idea of getting home late because she thinks it's not safe out there. I found this kind of ironic because our past campaign in YOHANA was "pedestrian and night safety" which applies to everyone in the community.

I have been to a lot of meetings in YOHANA. Before each meeting we always have an agenda written on the board and that agenda will be followed. We start with a question to get to know how everyone is doing. Then, we do an icebreaker to get the members together. Then, we get going to the important stuff like this open mic we host. At the end, we will do this thing called *Isang Bagsak,* a Tagalog phrase which roughly means "Unity Clap." We do it after the meeting to show that we successfully went over something, went over a problem, or resolved an issue, and we're now ready to get on to the next one together.

In one of the meetings, we had an Educational Discussion (ED) about the Central SOMA Plan. SOMA means South Of Market Area and the plan is going to displace a lot of families in the neighborhood because it introduces 33,000 new tech jobs and only 8,300 housing units. They also informed us about a public appeal against the Central SOMA Plan at City Hall. We were then given sentence starters and more information about the plan. Then, I composed my speech for the Board of Supervisors. I had a little trouble writing my speech because it was my first time doing something like that; facing the Board of Supervisors and having them actually listen to what I said was big. I spent a few days on my speech and I also practiced it a lot. The day of the public appeal, I was nervous. Very nervous. When I was in the line waiting to speak to the Board of Supervisors, my hands were shaking as I silently practiced my speech over and over. I had never been in this situation before, with people from different places listening to me. And it was also going to be televised somewhere. But as I was giving my speech, I felt great. All the nervousness came off and adrenaline boosted my energy. After my appeal, I felt accomplished. I did something that could possibly prevent the people in the community from getting evicted or worse.

"After my appeal, I felt accomplished.
I did something that could possibly
prevent the people in the community from
getting evicted or worse."

This summer was a turning point in my life. It made me a better individual and all the experiences that I had taught me how to be an effective leader and community member. This experience also introduced me to new opportunities for what I could do in the future. I used to imagine that I could only be in those traditional jobs like doctor, nurse, and engineer. Now, I realize that the selection of careers is more complex than what I thought it was, and that I actually have more choices now than the standard path. I was introduced to a lot of new friends that I can talk to when I have problems in school, my life, or even love. Additionally, I now have new mentors who I can look up to. Overall, this summer was a blast and it made me a better person. It introduced the world to a new version of me, a better and more knowledgeable version of Adriel.

---

**Adriel N.** *was born in the Philippines. He's sixteen years old. He likes basketball and now plays for the school's varsity football team. One day, he hopes to become an inspiring pilot and travel to different places. He likes mostly every food except seafood, because he's allergic to it.*

# OVERCOMING CHALLENGES

—

## JIAYI O.

When I first came to the United States, I went to a school called Chinese Education Center. As I walked into the school, no one was wearing uniforms. This was very different from the schools in China. When I walked into the classroom, everyone was speaking English and I didn't understand what they were saying. The kids were playing some board games I'd never seen before. Already, day one, I felt like I was fresh off the boat. I was like the only one in the land who was alone, while everyone was forming a group of people. Everything looked different and I felt like I had entered a totally different world.

Two of my Chinese classmates were playing a game that looked very fun. I was so relieved to see people like me who I thought I might be able to talk to. I asked in Chinese if I could join them, assuming they spoke Chinese too, but then quickly realized they spoke a different dialect. I thought I'd formed a pathway to communication, but even that small road had major cracks.

Later on, the bell rang. Everyone was sitting down and ready for the class to begin. I was the only one standing awkwardly in front of the class. I was scared because everyone was staring at me like some alien from another planet. They were silently whispering to each other, but it felt like they were shouting into a microphone. And unlike schools in China, the class size was very small so I couldn't be anonymous;

there was no blending in. I felt nervous because their faces didn't wear welcoming expressions; their cold eyes said to go away. I had never seen such looks before. I surveyed the classroom from afar and saw no open seats. I wanted to dig a hole and bury myself in it. As the teacher told me to introduce myself, my body was shaking like there was an earthquake. I didn't know what to say and didn't know how I was supposed to introduce myself.

Finally, the teacher assigned me to sit next to a Chinese girl that was from Taishan. I felt a bit calmer because the girl looked nice and kind, and she taught me a lot. Her name was Susan, and we began working together almost every day. She would help me with school work and explain things to me. She started to become a friend, almost like a big sister to me. I felt like I was skydiving and had attached myself to her parachute.

## "I thought I'd formed a pathway to communication, but even that small road had major cracks."

When I wasn't with Susan, I was alone on an island. During lunch time, everyone was playing in the yard. Kids were yelling across the yard. Some of them were laughing and they seemed like they were having a lot of fun. Some of the girls were whispering to their friends and sharing jokes. The yard was very hot; it was hot enough that I couldn't even breathe. I was trying to join one of the dodgeball groups, but they didn't seem like they wanted me to join them. Literally, I was suffocating from the heat, but I was also suffocating from my feeling of aloneness. I felt left out, so I went to sit on the bench.

Day after day, I worked to make new friends, but for some reason, not many of my classmates liked it. I think it was because they didn't know me that well. Sometimes when some of my classmates were having a conversation and I tried to join them, they ignored me. In order to make myself be part of the group, I always learned to communicate with them. My classmates were like water and I was like ice that takes time to melt and become water.

It was almost the end of the school year. I felt proud because I realized that I had overcome so many of the challenges throughout the entire year. As summer was approaching, I felt excited by the possibility of travel and getting away from the pressure of school and trying to fit in. One day after school toward the end of the school year, I raced home anxious to ask my mom what adventure or travel we had planned over the summer. When we lived in China, we would always travel around and visit my grandma. This was something I looked forward to, and I couldn't wait to go on an adventure, relax, and forget all the difficulties I had throughout the school year. But to my utter disappointment, my mom told me we would spend the whole summer at home; we were going nowhere. My heart sank and I started to cry on the bed.

During summer I was bored, so I tried to watch some English movies to improve my English. I had nothing to do, so I went to the park and my newfound confidence in English allowed me to meet new people. After this, the summer didn't go as badly as I thought it would, and I also gained some good things, like friends.

Seventh grade was a turning point for me. I was at the point where I felt more open to making new friends. I started to hang out with some other people who didn't speak Chinese or have the same dialect as me. I realized that I could learn something, and that they were also willing and open to teach me. As the time went on, my English improved and I was able to communicate with anyone.

I'm now a tenth grader, and these challenges that I've been through have pushed me further than I thought I was capable. I realize now that I have overcome so many challenges that have made me stronger as a person. I have gained so much strength and acquired new relationships that have helped me cross the border to the other side. The ice of the glacier has melted, and I have become water that can assimilate into anything and anyone I want. I couldn't see from the beginning, when I used to be a person who didn't speak any English and had no friends at all, that I would become a person who feels confident to meet new friends and communicate with anyone.

———

*Jiayi O. was born in Guangdong, China and is fifteen years old. She has a little sister. Her sister loves ballet. Jiayi loves to sing and she goes to karaoke every Sunday. She also loves to hang out with her friends. Her favorite sports are volleyball and basketball. She hopes to graduate in the United States and be a teacher in China after she graduates. She used to be an intern at the Mayor's Youth Employment and Education Program (MYEEP), a program that helps you to prepare for your future, and she loved to interact with the kids. Her favorite food is ice cream.*

# THOUGHTS ONTO PAPER

—

**PRETTY S.**

Since I was younger, around kindergarten, I always had an interest in art. Whether it was painting makeup on my dolls' faces, or drawing similar but jagged replicas of cartoon characters, I always found a way to express myself. It always made me feel more confident and it was a way to visually display my thoughts. Every Friday, I would be so happy to get my hands stained with various colors during art class, while a lot of the other kids were just happy to miss our math class for that day. I always would admire the not-so-perfect graffiti-covered walls around the city and the unique amount of artistic expression my mom and I would see out of the corners of our eyes walking around the Mission/Valencia District. I always felt like art was a strong way of showing who you are to the world; it's what makes you different from everyone else.

Experience. The word that always bothered me. The thing I thought I had to have to be the person I wanted. The word that haunted my everyday life. Can you be an artist without experience? Teaching? I don't know. But I did have "experience" in a certain sense. Life experiences, not just the cherry-picked, sugar-coated best moments of my life. Something to base my art off of, and that's plainly my life—whether it's mourning, happiness, or some sort of pain—I think of it all as experience. After all, without it I don't know where I'd get my inspiration from. I think I put myself into every art piece I create; it's created from emotion. It's created from that feeling of pain you have where you can't seem to stop the flow of tears and emotion pouring out from your heart. It's created from that feeling you get where you're so exuberant and overwhelmed with happiness that you can't stop smiling, laughing. So, this is my experience: the memories I have locked up in my head of who I am. Is that enough to paint the Mona Lisa? Well...not spot on, but I think that's just because of the type of life I've chosen to live.

My biggest inspiration ever since I was little has probably been my dad. My dad is an artist and a musician, and he raised me around a lot of punk rock music and artwork. My dad's work and his life always made me feel like I could accomplish my goals. He told me that since he started his first band he wanted to get signed to SST Records, a famous record company, and in the end, he accomplished his dream. It made me feel like if he could do it, I could do it. My dad always was there to help critique my art; he always had a suggestion. It could be frustrating sometimes, being a little girl who just sketches anime characters and Powerpuff Girls, my dad would always tell me to fill the page up. I didn't really feel like my cartoons were appreciated. I felt this wall between who I wanted to be and who I really was. I wanted to get enough guidance to find myself. That was before I developed my own style. I was still learning how to draw, so his constructive criticism wasn't always so clear to me. I always knew my dad was an artist. I would see the weird, complicated pieces hung up in the hallway of our house, the type of artwork that made you think. Complicated detail so small it almost tricked your eye for a scribble. I wanted to know how to do it. How could I fill a page with my thoughts alone, with no help from anyone else?

Music has always been a heavy influence for me. When I was six, I started playing piano, flute, and singing. I liked to play piano, but in my lessons, I always felt like I had to stay in the box. I couldn't ever make my own music, like the music my dad always had playing around the house. I didn't have the access to discover my own music as a girl in elementary school. Most of the time I would be listening to whatever would be spinning around the record player. As I got older and I started developing my own taste for music, when drawing or working on a piece I would always have something playing in the background. "Psycho seventy-eight, talkin' bout', twelve o'clock, don't be late. All this horror business, my mirrors are black!" I would sharpen my pencil, then sing along to whatever was playing, whether it was the Misfits or something like the Addicts. "*Viva La Revolution!*" I feel like people develop who they are, their character, based off of music. And since character develops from music taste, could my art be influenced by music? When I'm drawing, if something dark starts playing, I feel like I'm in that kind of mood. If something happier turns on, I'll feel more excitement and whatever I'm drawing might change. The outcome of my work always depends on the mood I'm in and the kind of music playing around me.

Art has always been something I've been confident in. No matter what, it never judges you, you can spill your thoughts and feelings onto paper. You can be who you want to be through art. It always has been an alternate world, a place where I decide what goes where, when I tell a story visually. On the inside, I feel like everyone has a voice in their consciousness telling them what's right and wrong in a social situation. In a way, you're the biggest influence on yourself and you create borders for yourself based on the way you feel and who you think you are. When it comes to self-expression though, I feel like you can come out of the box that society labels and traps you in. You can show what you're interested in and what impact you want to leave on the world through art.

---

*Pretty S. was born in San Francisco. She is fifteen years old. She likes to play music and make psychedelic art pieces. One day, Pretty has hopes of becoming a nurse while continuing her pursuit of art. Overall, she wants to express herself through music and art, hopefully gaining the support of others.*

# FINISH ON THREE

—

## WEN S.

As the ball comes up the court, I hear my teammates yelling, "Screen right!" The coach calls my name. I go to the middle and kneel down, knowing that I'm getting put into the game.

I hear the loud whistle chirping and the referees say, "Subs, come in." When the opponent misses, I get the rebound and dribble up the court. With a hard dribble I drive in, and I get fouled. The referee says, "Two shots." On that free throw line, I get nervous. It is my first time ever shooting free throws.

As I lined up my feet on the free throw line, I felt very light. The crowd in the gym was silent. I could feel their stares piercing through me. I bounced the ball three times. Feeling as nervous as I was, I shot it. The ball felt very light so I didn't flick it as hard as I usually would. The ball flew in the air, not even hitting the backboard. I felt embarrassed. My hands started to get more and more sweaty. I glanced at my coach and he said, "Take your time, just imagine that the audience isn't here." I got ready for the second shot, lining my feet back up. I bounced the ball three times again. I raised my arms up and shot the ball. This time, the ball hit the rim and almost went in. After those free throws, I was beginning to feel more nervous.

I started playing in organized leagues when I was very young and my teammates were not as experienced as I was. For many of them, it was their first season. It was only our third game of the season and we didn't feel like a team yet. To most of them, it was their first time playing in an organized league instead of just recreational ball. I really did enjoy them as people, but playing with them was difficult and frustrating. They made stupendous plays, but lost the ball very often.

I was beginning to feel more nervous. The confidence I had before suddenly wasn't there anymore. The whistle chirped. *Brrrrrrrrr.* Coach called a timeout and he was so supportive toward the team. He encouraged us to stay positive and to finish out the quarter strong. I was not the only one who was nervous. Most of my teammates were also nervous because of their inexperience playing in an organized league. We all put our hands in the middle and our captain said, "Finish on three!" We were starting to feel more confident.

We played great and we played hard. In the second half, I felt like our play styles really bonded us together. Earlier in the season, it was hard to play with them, but as we played more and more I adapted to the way they played. However, we lost the game because of something we couldn't yet control. Being nervous is a regular feeling and I know it won't affect us in the future. To me it doesn't matter if we win or lose the game, but it matters if my teammates and I achieve a goal we have been working on. We might've lost this game, but we will definitely be stronger as a team due to our strong bonds.

---

*Wen S. was born in San Francisco. He is fifteen years old. He likes to play video games. He wants to start a business or be a part of a company one day.*

# COOKER ANDY

—

## LARRY T.

Andy Candy was a normal guy who was born to cook. His mom and dad were both Chinese immigrants. He didn't talk to them much. His mom didn't have a job and his dad worked as a car mechanic. He had a brother called Ivan who was three years older than he was, and they were really close siblings. They lived in a small apartment in Chinatown, San Francisco.

When Andy was five years old, his parents took him out to a nice Chinese restaurant and this was a moment that would change his life forever. When Andy and his family walked in, Andy was amazed. He smelled the garlic, ginger, and soy sauce and saw all the wonderful dishes that chefs had prepared. He saw the nice cream-colored chairs and tables. He sat down on his chair and he was very happy. His mom ordered a plate of beef fried rice and Andy was curious. The fried rice looked perfect, each grain of rice perfectly laid out on the plate. Andy grabbed a spoon and began putting the rice on his plate. He took a bite and his taste buds felt like a kid getting candy. He loved the rice. Everything about the rice was perfect; the taste, the texture, the looks, and the smell were perfect. He then finished up the whole plate of rice by himself. When they went home he begged his brother to show him pictures of fried rice on the family computer and he did. That made Andy feel like he was in heaven. After this moment, Andy started cooking and watching the Food Network.

When Andy started elementary school, he wasn't the best student. He wasn't the smartest or the most likeable person. He had no friends and everyone called him fat because he liked to eat. He was picked on the most by this kid called Bob. Bob always had to show Andy that he was worse at everything single thing compared to him. One time, Bob and Andy agreed that they would do a cooking battle where they would have the teacher taste and decide which one of their foods was better. So, on the day of the battle, Bob brought his plain white boiled eggs and Andy brought his California roll that he made himself. He sliced the cucumber at home slowly and perfectly. He had perfectly placed the crab and rolled the roll. Andy thought that this time he could beat Bob at something. The teacher tasted both of their foods and the teacher picked Bob and his eggs because the teacher didn't like sushi, but Andy never knew this. This devastated Andy that he lost to Bob in something he practiced and spent so much time on. After this, he hated school and the only thing he looked forward to was going home to cook, but that got depressing because each time he cooked he would remember Bob beating him. He lost confidence in cooking. Andy cooked dinner for his family and they said they loved the food that he cooked for them, but he knew that they were faking it. Andy started drifting away from his family at this point. Ivan was the only person at the time that helped Andy with his problems. Andy wanted to be like Ivan.

Andy later graduated from elementary school and moved on to middle school. He still had no friends and the worst thing for Andy was that Bob was still picking on him for being fat. Andy now had improved his cooking a lot, to the point where he had the skill to quit school and become a full-time chef, which he did think about. He wanted to quit, but his brother would always encourage him to not give up. Andy continued to go to school, but his grades were not good. Every day in school, Andy put his head down in class and thought about all the different dishes he could make.

In eighth grade, the bullying got worse as Bob now had a gang of friends who were loyal to him. Andy was getting depressed, because school was hard and he had no friends. He felt alone because his brother had gone to high school and was focused more on studying than helping Andy. One morning at school, close to summer break, he told himself today was his last day on Earth. He had given up on his dream of being a chef. Once he got home, he was going to end his life. Then someone walked up to him. It was a new student. It was a girl. The girl asked him where this class on her schedule was and Andy told her. She thanked him and she walked away.

Andy went to math class and sat down in his seat. He was alone at the table because no one wanted to sit with him. Then the girl from earlier walked in and talked to the teacher. The teacher told her she could sit anywhere she wanted. The girl then sat down right next to Andy. Her name was Sandy. She introduced herself to Andy and Andy couldn't believe it. He was actually having a conversation with a girl. Andy told her that he liked cooking and she said she liked cooking, too. The bell rang and they went to lunch and kept talking. School eventually ended and they said goodbye. Andy went home that day the happiest he had ever been. He felt that he finally had a friend for the first time.

They kept talking with each other at school and soon they became close friends. Andy's grades rose from the ashes of hell as he actually felt school was important and also got help from his brother. On the final days of school before summer break, Sandy told Andy that her dad owned a restaurant that wasn't doing so well and that he could work there as chef for the summer to help boost their customers. Andy happily accepted.

On the first day of the job, he walked in and saw Sandy. He didn't only see her, but he saw Bob there. Andy immediately asked her what Bob was doing there and she told him that Bob was her cousin. Andy thought about it and realized that Bob was the boss' nephew. Bob then told Andy that they were now coworkers and they should work together.

The days passed as they fed the customers who came into the restaurant. Then one day, Sandy's dad had an important announcement to make. He told the workers that there was going to be a food reviewer coming in two days and told everyone to think about a plate they wanted to make. Everyone went home and thought about what they were going to make. Andy thought long and hard about it, but he didn't know what to make.

The day came when the reviewer was going to come. The restaurant closed early as they were preparing for the reviewer. Everyone knew what they were going to make except Andy. The reviewer was there. He was a very fancy man and seemed very gentleman-like. The older chefs started cooking their dishes and each time they went out, they came back in as if he didn't even eat it. Even the boss's dish was sent back. All the chefs went except for Bob, Sandy, and Andy. Bob made fried chicken and sent it out. One minute later, it came back in. Now it was Sandy's turn. She made some scrambled eggs and sent them out. The reviewer looked at the bowl and smacked it off of the table. The bowl rolled around the floor and the eggs got all dirty. He asked to see who made this and she went out. He told her that her dish was so bad he didn't even have to taste it to know it was bad. She started crying and ran back to the kitchen. Andy saw this and he was sad. It was his turn. The fate of the restaurant was all on him. The restaurant needed a good review. Bob told him, "Hurry up, Fatty."

Then something inside Andy clicked like police pulling the trigger on a bad guy. He told him to shut up. The atmosphere changed completely and the kitchen went silent. Andy thought of what had just happened to the person who saved him from his depression and even got him the job. He thought about all the struggles he went through. He knew what he was going to make. He was going to make a plate of beef fried rice. His body moved; it felt like it was moving by itself and his movements were unrealistic. He was doing everything perfectly. He was a one hundred percent tryhard. He finished and sent it out. The reviewer looked at it. His eyes sparkled and he took a bite. He stopped eating elegantly and started eating like a pig. The dish was perfect like a perfect circle. The reviewer got up, walked to the kitchen, and thanked him for the food. A few days later, the newspaper came and in the food section they found that the restaurant was rated ten out of ten. Andy was fully happy now. After all the mental obstacles he had to face, he now single-handedly saved a restaurant. Andy then decided to one day open up a Chinese restaurant that somehow helped people face depression.

---

*Larry T. was born in San Francisco and is sixteen years old. He is Chinese. He loves to play video games. In the future, he wants to be a pro-gamer.*

# A LETTER FOR A
# FUTURE MUSICIAN
—

### TINA W.

My friend Tina,

Hey Tina, it is so nice to meet you. I believe that you are taking care of the time difference right now. It is tough to spend thirteen hours on a plane, I know that. Oh, I forgot to introduce myself. You must be wondering who I am. My name is Tina, too. How wonderful that we share the same name! I came to the U.S. at the same time you did. Coincidentally, we also took the same flight.

I am writing to you for a reason. Shhhh, let me tell you a secret: I…am…a prophet! And I saw that something bad is going to happen to you. Wait! I can prove myself. Please hear me out. "Do you know where the exit is?" Memorize this sentence because you are going to be lost in the huge labyrinthine-like airport in five minutes. A security guard will come to you and ask you if you need any help. Just don't be embarrassed (again). Now you believe me, don't you? You are in big trouble!

Let me tell you a story: long, long ago, there was a little girl named Qiwei. She was very talented in music, and for that reason, she loved music. When Qiwei was ten years old, she found out that people who could play the keyboard were so cool. She begged her mom to go to a keyboard class. Anyway, this enthusiasm did not last long. She started believing that becoming a keyboard player was childish and ridiculous. There were a whole lot of professional keyboard players! *How was it possible that I could exceed them or even be one of them?* she thought. She quit immediately, so no more time would be wasted. She had tried so hard to get rid of her love for music, but there was just no way to get that simple, easy job done. A few months later, she got into middle school. Her music teacher showed her a piece of music that was played by the flute. The tone was clear as a creek, beautiful and flowing from her head to toes. She loved that sound, and she was inspired to go to flute classes. Qiwei was really talented on flute. She passed the level eight test in her first year of learning flute with a perfect grade. Eventually, she realized how this whole thing was even more childish and ridiculous. Being a musician? Impossible, unrealistic.

After several years, she followed her family's wish and got a normal, regular job. By chance, Qiwei came across biographies of successful musicians who had similar stories to the younger and wishful Qiwei. Only, these successful musicians actually followed their dreams of playing music. They shared their stories and told the world what a difference one single choice could make. Qiwei felt regretful that she didn't do the same. She chose to follow her family's wishes, but hid hers inside of her heart. She wished to go back in time so she could walk the right path true to her heart. It was all too late…

Pathetic. I feel sorry for Qiwei, but more angry, too. Why didn't she hold fast to her dreams? Why not follow her heart? Why be normal?

Your life is yours. How long can a life be? Eighty years? Ninety years? No doubt, life is short and time flies. A day with sadness is a day; a day full of joy is also a day. Why don't you live every day happily? Why don't you live your life the way you want it to be? You must be fourteen years old right now, am I right? You think you are so young, that you still have time to decide which way you want to go for your future? No! You have to start thinking about it right now, start thinking at this moment. It is never too early to start thinking about your future. You can't run away from this decision and neither can I. If you chose the life that your family assigned you, I mean, of course you can do that if you want to, but would you ever be happy?

Imagine this: you wake up every morning when no one is awake. Like a thief, you are afraid of making a single small sound, because you could interrupt your family's dream for you: that their daughter finally achieved the dreams that they themselves were unable to fulfill. You drag your tired body to the cold, quiet office, working the job that you have no interest in.

Would this life make you happy? What is realistic, even? Reality is what people create, not what God gives us. It can be changed. Stop acting like you're in a cocoon, crouched in a barrier that you made. Protect the tiny, weak dream hiding in the deepest, darkest corner of your heart. Protect the reality you think it is. Protect your power, your ability, your possibility. Protect the true…you.

Your dream, Qiwei's dream, my dream. These dreams are not immature. Break out of the cocoon, and be reborn as the musical butterfly you always wanted to be!

Best,
Tina

———

*Tina W. was born in Zhejiang, China, which is a small beautiful town near Shanghai. She is sixteen years old and is a sophomore in Galileo High School. She moved from China to the U.S. in April 2017. She likes many things, such as drawing and the flute. She loves sweets, so she started baking and found out it brings her so much fun. Her dream is simple: that she and her family could have a happy life together.*

# UNALIKE

—

**ANSON W.**

Being a first-generation Asian American has been a border for me my entire life. It was difficult growing up trying to live an "American lifestyle." The "American lifestyle" is painted throughout national television, where you see white folks and their children running around in big houses, going to exciting places like amusement parks and big parties, and eating "American" foods like cheeseburgers or ice cream. I didn't grow up in a perfect two-story, five-bedroom house with five family members. I didn't wake up every early morning to the sweet aroma of blueberry pancakes sizzling on the stove. I didn't race bicycles down the block with all my friends. We didn't celebrate Halloween carving spooky faces into big orange pumpkins, or Christmas hanging up big, red, and round ornaments on a tall green Christmas tree.

My parents are both immigrants from China. They came here a little under twenty years ago. My dad could speak English, but not very great, while my mom still can't really speak it. Growing up I was raised in an old, yellowish, booger-colored house. It was two stories with a plain backyard filled with dead brown flowers and a cracked cement ground, a rusty metal shed that squeaked every time you opened it, and an oddly tall fruit tree that produced juicy, gold-colored loquats. Our family was made up of twelve people, from our grandparents to us little toddlers. Bedrooms jam-packed with clothes and toys, a living room where babies cried, where dinner was served, where the entire family sat together to enjoy TV. I grew up with the tradition of receiving red envelopes for Lunar New Year and lanterns and mooncakes during Mid-Autumn Festival. This is what I grew up with, and this is what made me different from everyone.

I was always treated differently from others. For example, I noticed this throughout my early years in school. My friends' families spoke English and mine didn't, so they would always point that out, embarrassing me. Everyone always had pizza or sandwiches for lunch, while I always had rice. My friends always wore nice clothes from the mall, but I always had on clothes that my family got from China. All the kids played kickball and had video game consoles, but my hands were always full of storybooks and crayons. I never really blended in with everyone. My lifestyle was too different, and I always tried to hide it.

I had many ways of covering up who I was. I never invited anyone over to my house because I didn't want my friends to think I was weird for how different I was from them. I would eat by myself or throw away my lunch so I wouldn't get noticed eating something people had never heard of. Whenever someone brought up what I was wearing, I would blush and try to change the subject.

As a kid, I had low self-esteem. I felt like I couldn't relate to anyone and that I didn't fit in. There was no group that I felt like I belonged to. My entire early life was spent just trying to fit in. Trying to be like everyone and live like them was my way of trying to overcome the border.

I remember nagging my dad for things that I saw my friends had, from a Nintendo DS to a clean pair of Nike Free RNs. I don't think my dad understood how I felt, so he never listened and never bought me anything. It was always, "Focus more on school," or "Buy things you need." Unlike me, my dad grew up in an environment where families were raised similarly. He grew up in a village in China, where everyone grew up working in fields, where the kids ran around in the woods and nearby lakes catching bugs and small animals, and where everyone was basically the same. They all spoke the same language, lived around each other, went to the same school, were the same race, and shared the same culture. He could never understand how different it was for me. Home to him was the place you grew up in, a place where the tradition stayed the same, where the word "different" wasn't mentioned.

Something I decided to do was to act like the other kids. I started playing a lot of different sports and I am glad I did. Whenever my friends and I played sports, from kickball to football, I always felt like I belonged with them. I was able to have fun and enjoy myself without considering myself to be the odd one out. One specific thing I picked up was basketball. It started as an activity during recess and became a big commitment in my life—and still is to this day. I still love the sport of basketball and continue to play almost every day.

To this day, I still feel like I am treated differently. But my way of overcoming this border is accepting it. I've realized that everyone is different and you should live according to your own identity. Trying to be like someone you are not is hard, almost impossible. Sure, this border kept me separated from some people, but some borders aren't meant to be crossed.

———

*Anson W. was born in San Francisco and is fifteen years old. He likes to play basketball and listen to music. He hopes to go to college and work with computers. His favorite basketball player is Devin Booker.*

# DANDELION

—

**ELIZABETH W.**

A white dandelion in a field of flowers.
The pale glow that stands out
and without a doubt,
I'm different.

Take a look and you will see
I may stand out subtly.
My light skin and blonde hair
in a field of opposites.

Words carry in the breeze
and the dandelion is me.
The flower is fragile:
soft fibers easily flee.

Uncommon, uncertain,
a loneliness.
There aren't many dandelions
in this field of flowers.

Make a wish to myself
to feel more content
and have acceptance
that I am different.

Fuzz flies away,
a rebirth of seeds.
Planted in the ground,
I will be free.

A new beginning, a realization.
Almost away from the fear of not fitting in.
An indication
that even though our roots may differ,
in the end, we are in the same soil.

————

*Elizabeth W.* *was born in Thailand. She is fifteen years old. She likes to play tennis and listen to music. When she is older, she would love to travel the world.*

# GROWING OUT OF MY CORNER

—

## CAIYAN Y.

On a sunny day, I was outside in the courtyard of my high school waiting for my friend to arrive. I was sitting on a wooden bench, playing on my phone and daydreaming about when high school ends. I was thinking about living on my own and developing as an independent person when I finish high school. I won't have to listen to my parents constantly comparing me with others and making me feel like I am not good enough for them. I will get to make my own choices, like selecting food and classes that I enjoy. I will be able to eat pizza anytime and stay in chemistry class as long as I want. As I looked around the courtyard, there were other students like me and a lone tree. The tree reminded me of being outside and how much I enjoy my favorite walk on a path surrounded by trees. The scenery there is so much more exciting than at school. Just like me though, the lone courtyard tree was trapped in the corner of many buildings.

I was sixteen years old with messy and tangled black hair. I saw myself as a broken mirror and hated when others looked at me. I couldn't perceive what others saw in me. I wore generic shoes, while others wore brand-name shoes. I wanted others to stop paying attention to me and concentrate on themselves. I felt like my older siblings were just nice to me because I was their little sister. In school, my history scores were horrible. I felt like I would never be good at history. I just couldn't get my mind interested in history like it was in chemistry and math. I felt like a villain, blaming everything on the teacher for not teaching me well. I was frustrated and annoyed, thinking that I would never improve.

As I look up from my phone that day, my best friend is walking toward me with her hair tied back in a ponytail. My best friend is different from me because she is more outgoing and way more confident than I am. I am an introvert and depend on others very often. I depend on her to make me happy. Whenever I need help, I ask her instead of the teachers. She is always there for me and really helpful. She always encourages me to be more open and confident. She makes my mirror feel less broken because she makes me think I am much better than what I think of myself. She always has a smile on her face. She makes my sophomore year happier than it would otherwise be.

"Hi! How are you doing?" she asks.

"I'm fine. The teacher posted the grades for the chemistry test. How did you do on it?"

She shrugs. "I did worse on the previous test I took."

"How bad was it? Is it a 'B' or an 'A'?"

"I got a 'B' this time. I feel sad. I wish I could've done better," she replies.

"It's fine. You can do better next time." I feel really bad for getting an 'A' so I tell her that I also got a 'B.'

She says, "Stop lying. You probably got an 'A'. You are smarter than me."

I don't deserve the compliment because there are so many smarter students out there. I dislike being complimented and want her to stop praising me. Even when I do a little better, she keeps on saying positive things about me. I feel annoyed because she does it so often that I have become immune to her compliments. I am not sure how to respond to her telling me that I'm lying about my grade because I want to encourage her to feel good about herself, but on the other hand, I actually did better than she did.

Whenever I acknowledge that she is better than I am in other classes, she denies the truth. Sometimes I lie to be encouraging. My brother also lies to make me feel better. I lie to my friend about my grades and my friend lies to me by denying that she is better than I am in English. For me, lies and the truth have become hard to differentiate. I don't always know whether to believe the positive things people say to me.

I am trapped by my lack of self-confidence just like the tree is trapped inside the school's courtyard. The tree is permanently trapped like me. I want to exit through the door far away, but the idea of getting good grades pulls me back into the corner. I'm just not confident enough and my horrifying grades are tearing me apart. The barrier is so visible to me that I can see it in front of my eyes. Every day I fear that I will see the dark, scary barriers again. I can't take in any compliments from my best friend because all the expectations and desire for perfection are killing me. I am screaming from the inside, but smiling on the outside. The situation is better in history class. I got a better score on my last tests. However, I still always expect an 'F.'

Like the tree, I am afraid I will never grow because I'm always stuck in the corner and can never get out to grow my confidence. I want to be different from the tree because I want to leave my corner and find myself. I hope in the future I can get out of my comfort zone and become more confident. I want to change my history and become someone new in the future.

———

*Caiyan Y. was born in China and is sixteen years old. She has three older brothers. She loves to watch dramas. Her favorite food is combo pizza. One day, she hopes to become a successful person. She is in high school and is looking forward to college.*

# IN BETWEEN
—

# INTRODUCTION

—

## K.R. MORRISON

*ENGLISH TEACHER AT GALILEO HIGH SCHOOL*

In fourteen years of teaching, the personal stories of my students continue to breathe stronger than grades, district tests, and school district expectations. My formula has been simple but my process always proves complex, and never on my watch. Meet each and every student where they're at. Show students I see them, and that they're worth positive expectations. Most of all, stay a student myself, and demonstrate on the daily that I love this splendid craft I teach—the magic of words, and the art of writing and reading literature. Somehow in the precious Tetris between us, our roles in room 462 intertwine until their *own* words come, unraveling restless stories waiting in their backbones, begging to be told.

I'm blessed to be a part of such a process, witnessing how words can rescue young people the same way they saved me from my own dark contexts, a lifetime ago. Before my students open a book, I ask them to consider the story elements of their lives. The settings into which they're born and endure, the antagonists and resulting conflicts that have shaped their worst moments and greatest triumphs, ancestor plots they inherit like relentless ghosts, or their protagonists that bring relief in an otherwise abusive American reality. To understand their own personal story elements begins the daunting process of self-transformation and thus, *writing their resolutions,* so to speak, and what better protagonist to enlist in that process than the written word. In this sense, words and writing tactics become the teachers, and my job is to nourish a space for writing to work its magic and from there, stay out of the way.

It is with such teaching strategies in mind that I view 826 Valencia as another kind of protagonist in my students' lives. This project created a space for my students' voices to stir and emerge, and through committed tutors and their writing toolboxes, my students were given the opportunity to explore the bruises on their hearts, or their own testimonies to the America they experience, for better or for worse. In the case of these young writers—a collective of different, yet ironically similar kids who often feel silenced—826 Valencia found and nurtured their voices into stories. In light of this, 826 Valencia is a kind of activist, a systematic challenger that combats an America that traditionally, profits from youth's indifference, silence, and social illness.

When asked what book I wanted to use as our focus, I had to go with yet another protagonist that's used my classroom to save students over the years—Luis Rodriguez's memoir, *Always Running.* What book manages to stay relevant after nearly fifteen years in the classroom? What book hooks students through riveting story, speaking to *all* teenagers who pass through room 462? What book saves lives, calls America's "story elements" into question, and after all these years, still continues to shape my curriculum regarding literary devices, poetry and prose, or the many windows into theme and an author's purpose? Every year, I've used this precious story in my classroom and every year, I'm awed by its relevance, by Rodriquez's dimensional balance of gripping story and artistic craftsmanship, and I'm not a bit surprised to discover how his book organically speaks to the many dimensions of borders that antagonize my students.

Borders. The word is hot right now, grounded in a political narrative that every day, makes or breaks student safety and their sense of self-worth. Under a leadership whose hands are bloody and a seemingly never-ending increase of hate crimes towards marginalized communities, San Francisco teenagers face threats and in some cases, direct acts of deportation and consequently, this current crime against humanity has become an American teenager's primary antagonist. For other students, their experiences with borders are more figurative. In all cases, however, borders seem to lead to the same situation but in different sceneries—abuse, internal conflict, and restrictions from self-acceptance and personal empowerment.

Through these student stories, I'm reminded that young people have something to say and a hunger to unravel the "story elements" into which they're born. Through these stories, I'm motivated to stay in the trenches, let words do the healing, give students the space and the magic books to write their way over walls and into self-love, on their *own* terms.

# A SHORT STORY
—

**M**y **ammo and** I were sitting on the porch of his house, looking over the view of the Ingleside houses. Due to the typically chilly weather of San Francisco, we were huddled in jackets, joking around about how different Americans were from us. In America, there is a vast amount of freedom. We could make fun of the president publicly and nobody would care. In Iraq, you would get arrested if you even whispered the name of the dictator. The majority fail to realize how open you can be here, from the right to protest and have free speech, down to what you can wear. My ammo and I have a very close relationship. He is like a dad to me, since mine left when I was very young. He would always take me out to the mall and buy me toys as a child. I never knew anything about his past until he told me all he had to sacrifice to get to be under the California sun instead of the war-torn place where he grew up.

He was born on July 1, 1970, in Al-Kūt, Iraq. The neighborhood he grew up in was bustling with people. It was a big city with *medinas,* which are a bunch of small stores bundled together. Growing up, his family was middle class. His memories of his mother are sparse due to her death when he was seven years old, while his father was notably open-minded, but got mad if he got bad grades or stayed out too late. His fondest memory is playing football (soccer in America) with his friends on the sand. My ammo started working at nine years old, selling plastic bags

105

on the street, compared to when I was nine, still playing with toys in the comfort of my own home. Husain was unproblematic—never got into a fight, never got bullied. Everyone in the neighborhood liked him. As a teenager he would hang out with his friends at cafes or at the movies. At fourteen years old, he acquired his first official job at a salon by lying about his credentials. When a customer eventually came to his booth, he didn't know how to cut hair and the result was horrible. His boss started to yell at him and he ran out, never to come back. When I was fourteen, I didn't even have a job since the legal working age here is sixteen. His next job was at a cafe, which didn't require as much previous experience. With hard work and side hustling by selling cigarettes, he was able to buy the cafe for himself at only sixteen years old. However, he had to sell the cafe once he was drafted into the war.

Under the rule of Saddam Hussein, every boy was drafted into the army at eighteen years old. My ammo and his friends were drafted once they graduated high school. Saddam Hussein was a very strict fascist ruler. His government could listen to phone calls and had propaganda everywhere. In the army, they woke up at four in the morning to exercise. Soldiers were forced to take off their clothes in the cold. Thankfully, it never snowed there. The worst experience he had in the army was when they would lay the soldiers on the floor and make them crawl across the floor.

One day, Ammo was driving home from the army base after staying at his base for months. He got stopped at a checkpoint, the United States Army's "Prisoner of War" camp in Saudi Arabia. First off, prisoners had to build their own tents in the middle of the desert. Guards were everywhere so he could not escape. They treated the prisoners badly. They would feed them like animals, throwing food onto the floor of the camp. Washing your clothes in a trash can was hard work. With a good behavioral record and a lot of luck, he was chosen by the U.S. to move to San Francisco.

Moving to America was nothing like he expected. He thought it would be easy, but it was not. Once 9/11 happened, he had to go through many years of hardship before actually becoming a citizen. Oh, how he was filled with joy when when he was accepted! Applying to move to America was one thing, but actually getting citizenship was a big thing. He packed his bags and never looked back. It was a nice view. The tall skyscrapers made him feel infinite, like anything was possible. Highways were long endless roads; the streets were packed with people of all colors and backgrounds. He felt like he would fit right in.

We walk back home. Standing on the same patio, I look back over to the view of the houses again. I realize how lucky I am to be born here. So many immigrants have fought for a long time here. I could not imagine doing the things that he has done. He has overcome the struggle and made it in the Golden City. I am lucky to have him in my life.

———

*Samia A.* *was born in San Francisco and is fifteen years old. She loves to play video games. She wants to be a doctor one day. Her favorite food is pizza.*

# THE VISIT

—

## MELANIE A.

Five minutes. I have felt as if my whole life has been in five minutes. Or shall I say my sixteen years of living on this planet have felt like five minutes. I would say the concept of time is irrelevant to me, but it is not. Five minutes is all you need to make an impulsive decision.

Take this as an example. One day in the middle of seventh grade, I came back from school and bought a plane ticket to Mexico and did not come back to San Francisco until three years later. You see, this decision was made in five minutes, with no previous thinking whatsoever. Or the time when I broke off my one-year relationship over text—that was done in five minutes. But this story is not about heartbreak or impulsive decisions (maybe). It's about something deeper…unconditional love.

As a kid I don't really remember much of my childhood with my mom, but instead with my abuelita. My abuelita. A strong woman who believed in the whole, "a woman does not need a man to provide for her. A woman can do it herself if she studies," concept. My mother believed quite the opposite, but that is beside the point. My abuelita: a woman with strong, calloused hands from years of hard working, yet still very feminine. She has *piel canela* that has gotten lighter throughout the years due to her being away from her warm *tierras*, skin always covered in gold. My abuelita has soft, yet dominating almond eyes that tell a story. Her thin lips have turned to a permanent scowl due to years of enduring hard struggles. Her laughs are rare, but they echo like the hollering of the mariachis at night. Her nose is not that of a common European, but a nose that that embraces her deep Mexican roots. Lastly, she has platinum straight hair that resembles that of a Mexican princess. This woman is called *Gloria*.

\* \* \*

I remember the times as a kid when my abuelita, my sister, and I would go to the park, or when she would take me to the doctors because I felt "sick." I also remember the times she would take me out for ice cream because I would be upset about the lack of my mother in my life, or when she would go to my field trips in kindergarten.

There was this one time in kindergarten when I begged my mom to go to a school field trip with me. How foolish of me. My mother refused, giving me the hard 'NO' and telling me she didn't have time for foolishness. I was five years old. I was beyond disappointed, but then again, it wasn't the first time she would reject me. But why did it hurt so much that one time? I proceeded to ask my abuelita, the woman who didn't speak or understand English, and without a doubt or a question she accepted to go on my field trip that took place in a beautiful strawberry field.

Funny enough, that wasn't the only time my grandma would accompany me on a field trip. She was always present at my school potlucks, dances, graduations, school meetings, and so on. It's a fact that my abuelita has always been there for my biggest life accomplishments, and for that I always made her Mother's Day cards or Valentine's Day cards school would make us do for our parents. I always made them directly for her.

With this being said, why is it that when I left to Mexico with my "mom," the woman who had never spared time for me in my childhood unlike my abuelita did, it was easy? At the time of departing from the woman who always had my back, it didn't even hurt, not one bit, and to this day, I hate myself for that reason alone.

\* \* \*

I'd like to think of my time in Mexico like a visit. You see, I've never considered it my home. My home has been and will always be Los Angeles or San Francisco, but never Mexico. And I will tell you why. The streets of Mexico were not like the streets I was accustomed to. They weren't smooth sidewalks with lights that illuminated every street, but rather cracked sidewalks with no stops signs.

Mexico was flat. There were no hills, no woods, no tall buildings that reminded me of skyscrapers, but rather poorly designed buildings that lacked fresh paint. When I went to Mexico, I had in mind it was a visit, nothing permanent. But boy was I wrong. Keep in mind this was the first time in thirteen years I would be living under the same roof as my mom.

And let me tell you, the first time I got there, I went to go hug the so-called figure who called herself "Mom." At that time, she had long black wavy hair that went all the way to her hips, and light tan skin that resembled coffee after you put in a bit too much milk. When I went to hug her, I was met with a quick hello and a "Hold on I have to talk to Luis." Luis was her current partner at the time. I didn't even get a hug, I was left standing there with my arms raised and my luggage by my side. And from that encounter only, I knew my stay in Mexico was going to be difficult.

———————

*Melanie A.* is a young Mexican American sixteen-year-old student who has lived in Mexico and has come back to the city of San Francisco. She has decided to tell about the ups and downs of her journey living in a different nation than she was used to.

# AMERICAN BLOOD

—

## NATALIE A.

Around a month before summer break of 2018, my family planned for my sister and me to go to El Salvador to visit our twenty-two-year-old brother Miguel. My sister at that time was nine years old and had never met my brother. And even though I was fifteen years old and had met my brother when I was much younger, I didn't have much memory of him. My brother Miguel was born in El Salvador and my sister Emelie and I were born in San Francisco, California. My parents left my brother with my grandparents at the age of two. Even though my parents knew that it was going to be hard to leave my brother with my grandparents, they couldn't provide for my brother or for themselves. So around twenty years ago, my mom made the decision to come to the United States. A year after my mom left, my dad came to the U.S. I imagine how excruciating it was to leave Miguel behind. My mom, Evelin, has always tried to be as close as possible to my brother by calling weekly; she still cared for him even if they were separated by thousands of miles. My sister and I were able to visit my brother because we were U.S. citizens, but my parents were not.

When my family booked plane tickets for me and my sister, I didn't know what to feel. Should I be excited? Should I be nervous? Should I feel sad because my parents hadn't seen my brother in around twenty years and they didn't have an opportunity to visit him? The day came quicker than expected. It was June 18, 2018. We left San Francisco to arrive in San Salvador.

After a six-hour flight, we finally arrived in San Salvador. When we got off the plane, we could feel the difference between a nicely air-conditioned plane and the humid and hot weather of San Salvador. We went through airport security and picked up our luggage, and my sister and I anxiously walked to the exit. It took us a while to find him, which made me think, *what if we get lost in an unknown country?* but I finally spotted him. In a way, I remembered meeting him before. When I saw him, I not only recognized him from seeing his pictures on Facebook, but I felt like I knew him. I wasn't really sure what to do. Should I hug him? Should I just say, "Hi, long time no see!" I am actually not sure what I did, but the next thing I remember is going on a four-hour drive to Cantón Las Charcas, the small village where Miguel lived.

When we arrived at his home, it was dark, so dark that you couldn't really see what was in front of you. My brother showed us to the room where we were staying and it was four concrete walls. The roof was wood planks with aluminum metal sheets, the floor was dusty packed dirt, and there was a single light bulb hanging in the middle of the room that as soon as you turned on the light, moths would come swarming. My brother had prepared a bed with a net-like canopy to protect us from the mosquitos. He told us, "You guys have American blood. Mosquitoes are attracted to your blood." I felt a bit bad for my brother because my sister and I slept in a bed and he slept in a hammock.

Throughout the two weeks we stayed there, we saw the differences between San Francisco and Cantón Las Charcas. Something my sister and I adapted to was the bathroom: to shower, you would use a bowl to pour water on yourself; there was a tank of water next to you and you would bring a bowl of cold water over your head. We could hear our brother tell us, "Don't use up all the water, because then you won't be able to shower tomorrow." Another thing was the food. You would often eat the same thing for weeks, like *pupusas* or red bean stew; fortunately, I brought apple and cinnamon instant oatmeal with me for breakfast.

After a while, I started to appreciate what I had back home. I also began to feel sadness not only because I missed my parents, but I also felt bad for my brother. Back home in San Francisco, my parents were always there for me and just thinking about my brother not having that made my eyes well up with tears. My brother had lived in his small village without us—his parents and sisters—almost all his life, and I started to feel like I already wanted to go back home after only two weeks away from my parents and the comfort I had at home.

When my sister and I came back from our trip to El Salvador, I remembered that Miguel had a chance to live with us in the United States, and I had a chance to have an older brother to protect me and someone to count on in rough times. Miguel's chance to live with us came about when a friend of my mom's told her that there was a program for young adults to come to the United States. This program was a legal program that allowed people of Central America who faced violence in their country to come into the U.S. My brother had many encounters with people who tried to jump him or introduce him to drugs and alcohol. So, my mother decided that we should apply for this program. After a few weeks we received a letter saying that he had been accepted. We knew that the process was going to take a few months, maybe even a year, but we had hope. The process of coming to the U.S. included evidence that showed that there was violence around him, an interview, a medical exam, and finally buying an airplane ticket for him to come to the U.S.

After around four months, he was finishing his medical papers when we received a letter that informed us that unfortunately the program was going to be terminated. At that point, my family was devastated. My brother was so close to being with us. The friend that had mentioned the program to us was able to bring her daughter to the U.S., even though she was not as far along in the process as Miguel. I didn't want to feel envious of my mom's friend's family, but I did feel that way. I wanted Miguel to be with our family, and that was taken from us. I wished Miguel could have had the opportunity to be the older brother that would protect me when someone would bother me, someone who

I could rely on in my darkest times, and be the someone to fight the battle of loneliness. Without Miguel here, I've missed out on getting the advice and help of an older brother, and when I struggle, I still wish he were here to answer my questions and show me how to grow up.

————

*Natalie A.* *was born in San Francisco. She is fifteen years old. She likes to play with her bunny and listen to music. One day, she wants to help people and give back to the community.*

# CONSEQUENCES

—

## HELEN C.

Ever since preschool, I've been really good friends with Maddie. We've never had the title of "best friends," but we knew that we could always trust each other and treat each other as if we were. We have a lot in common and share plenty of memories such as reading the *Magic Tree House* book series together, dancing to the *High School Musical* movies, and doing arts and crafts. We even live in the same neighborhood. Like all little girls, we dressed as if we were all set to go to My Little Pony's house. We would always dress in the colors of the rainbow. I always wore my favorite color, pink like cherry blossoms, and hers was lavender. We were so bright that others could possibly see us from a mile away. Other than all the cheerful memories, we did some mean things that led to negative consequences.

In elementary school, we bullied others knowing that consequences would come, but we were ignorant about how it would affect us. On a sunny afternoon during lunch, in the orange cafeteria with a red dragon poster hung up on the wall, I sat with Maddie. Taking in the smell of warm pasta were our two classmates who were Burmese and Russian. We knew that they couldn't understand the language that we spoke, so we decided to play a little game. Between the four of us, we played a game by answering "yes" or "no."

"Do you know what I'm saying?" I asked in Cantonese.

"No," one of them replied.

"Ohhh, they answered that correctly!" I said with excitement.

The game got more inappropriate when Maddie and I thought of a question, asking, "Do you wear clothes?"

Without understanding a word we said, they said "no" and we laughed.

Another girl, Katy, who sat across from us heard everything and snitched on us. She told the one teacher that everyone was afraid of, since she was that teacher's pet. From my nine-year-old memory, she looked like a scary woman with a mole on her face who would carry a clipboard around with her all the time.

"HELEN!" she shouted. "COME OVER HERE!"

With my little fearful self, I walked over there thinking, "Shoot, I'm doomed."

With her scary eyes staring at me, she questioned me, yelled at me, and pushed me, teaching me nothing but to hate her.

"So, Katy told me what you've done in the cafeteria. What made you do that, huh?" she shouted again.

I replied with, "It wasn't just me who was in on this."

"Well, I don't care. This isn't about someone else, it's about you right now!" she raised her voice.

I was speechless and filled with anger.

"Ugh, I can't believe you would do such thing," she added. "You listen to me, young lady. If you ever do that again, you will get in more trouble."

From there, she pulled my shirt and pushed me against the wall, giving me no mercy. I was furious. Tears falling. My friends, including Maddie, came out of the restroom and comforted me as they cried.

"Why are you crying?" I asked.

"Because I feel bad for you," they both said.

Before the teacher left, she threatened me, saying if I ever went near my friends or if they ever went near me, we would be punished. After everything happened, I felt as if the world flipped. I felt dizzy and my whole body felt weak. I cried and cried.

As a nine-year-old, and like many nine-year-olds would, I only focused on myself. All I cared about and wanted to do was to have fun and to avoid all these troubles. I would always hear the phrase, "Treat others how you want to be treated." That didn't get to me until recently. Last year, another friend of mine reminded me of how I was back in elementary school. She told me how I was very mean and a bully for planning to throw her water bottle in the garbage can with Maddie.

"You would always tell me to be 'it' in tag even when I didn't want to. You were really mean," she told me.

I felt my face turning into the color of a tomato. I was speechless and all I could say was "sorry." I thought over what she had said to me and I never realized that my actions had hurt others that badly. I'm glad that she opened up and shared the past with me because it made me more aware of my surroundings.

I know now that it's best to think before doing.

Bullying is something people would do for fun because it makes them feel good. I learned to respect others because there's so much that I don't know about what they're going through. It's important for everyone to understand how actions and words can hurt people. We don't need people to pity others, but to understand others. It's best for all of us to just treat others like how we want to be treated. The best way to avoid bad karma would be to stop the bullying. In the end, we're just humans who want to live happily.

---

*Helen C. was born in San Francisco. She is fifteen years old. She likes to play volleyball and has played for four years. She plans to return to track after a two-year break. She enjoys watching TV series and listening to pop music. Her favorite food is sushi and her favorite dessert is cookies and cream ice cream. She's always down to try new food. In her spare time, she hangs out with her friends. She is also looking forward to earning her own money to support herself.*

# DINNER WITH GRANDPARENTS

—

## ANDREW C.

Two or three years ago was when I became aware of the language
border between me and my relatives. The language border to me
was hard to overcome, like climbing a mountain. I realized this on the
weekend, either Saturday or Sunday.

Every year, we have special occasions like birthdays or whatever is
worth celebrating when my family and relatives gather for dinner. I
remember the day we went. It was raining lightly. The restaurant we
went to was big. It had a red-carpet floor with a high ceiling and was
a very spacious area. As we walked in, the steam of the salmon hit our
noses like a bus. Right when we entered, we could feel the warmth of
the restaurant. My family was like the first to get there, so we waited for
the others to arrive. As time passed, a lot of familiar faces I recognized
started walking in one by one and we all greeted each other. A tall man
like a redwood tree and a woman as tall as any other tree entered the
door. I instantly recognized them as my grandparents that I respect
a lot. I had not seen them for a month or so and because of that, my
grandparents came over and talked to me and others at the table. The
conversation was going well.

"Andrew, how are you doing in school?" they asked.

I told them I was doing well.

I understood what they were saying, but as the conversation carried on, I noticed I could understand less and less and was starting to get overwhelmed by what they were saying.

As I was thinking over what they were saying, the room became silent. I then realized that they were waiting for a response, but my mind went blank. I started to tense up like I had just woken up from a bad dream. The feeling of being confused made me feel uneasy, like getting called on in class to read to everyone in a language you are not fluent in. This feeling did not help me at all. I started to panic because it had been a while since someone had talked and I looked at my brother for help. But he seemed just as confused as I was, like we were getting asked for directions in a different country. Finally, the silence broke when my mom answered for me. My mom explained to them as to why I was not answering.

## "I started to tense up like I had just woken up from a bad dream."

"Sorry, they are not fluent in Chinese," said my mom.

Me and my brother are the only ones who are not fluent in Chinese in my family of four. We can still understand what people say, but when people talk fast, it gets harder for us to understand.

During the whole dinner, I was on my phone or talking with my cousins, who are fluent in English. We were talking about how school was going and other things that happened recently that were worth mentioning. The atmosphere was great—everyone was enjoying the food and each other's company. It was a bit awkward for most of the dinner for me, though, because of what had happened earlier. Nobody seemed to care about it, but during the whole dinner I was worrying about it and I was thinking of solutions to the problem I was having.

I came to the conclusion that I wanted to learn more about the language so I could communicate better with my relatives and something like that would not happen again. I started taking a Chinese language class and I've learned a lot of new things that I have used in conversations with my relatives. It feels great for me because it is like passing a test you studied hard for.

---

*Andrew C. was born in San Francisco. He is fifteen years old. He likes playing games and listening to music. He hopes to be successful in the future. He is a tenth-grade student attending Galileo High School. He does not have a favorite food.*

# CLOSED EYES

—

## PETER C.

It was the year 2014, September 1, my first day in the fifth grade. I stepped into the schoolyard feeling a mixture of excitement and nervousness. There was a crowd of little kids all huddled together in the schoolyard staring at the posters on the schoolyard walls. I joined the group of kids to see what was going on. It turned out the posters taped onto the tan schoolyard walls listed the classrooms students were assigned to. I glanced from paper to paper on the walls, struggling to find my name, when suddenly, the bell rang. I panicked as the crowd around me dispersed and disappeared into the school building. When I had finally found my name, the schoolyard was empty. I rushed to classroom 243, sprinting down the hallways and skipping stairs as I made my way to the classroom. I made it to class, out of breath, and opened the door.

My classmates had formed a circle around the room with my teacher, Ms. Thomas, standing in the middle. I spotted my best friend at the time, Victor, and joined him in the corner of the classroom.

"Alright class," Ms. Thomas said cheerfully. "Let's begin by sharing our names and a show we enjoy watching. Let's start with you," she said as she pointed her finger in my direction. My heart began to race as I opened my mouth to respond. Suddenly, a voice sprung up from beside me.

"Umm… My name's Victor and I like Pokémon." I was relieved that I was given more time to think as thoughts began to bounce around inside of my head.

"Oh, I love Pokémon!" Ms. Thomas exclaimed. "How about you, the boy in the light blue t-shirt standing next to Victor?"

"Okay," I said as I nervously glanced around the room. "My name is Peter and… I like Yu-Gi-Oh!"

"Sounds nice," Ms. Thomas said with a confused expression on her face.

A few months later in the schoolyard, Victor and I were sprinting across the yard, racing to get first in line for the daily handball games as we usually did. I was going fast, so fast in fact that I wasn't paying any attention to my surroundings and bumped into this dark-skinned girl, maybe a fourth grader, knocking the half-eaten pear out of her hand. Her brother, a kid an entire head shorter than me, jumped right on me, grabbing me by the collar of my shirt. He stood on his tippy-toes as he dug his nails into the front of my neck. "Hey!" he yelled. "Which one of you did that to my sister?" I chuckled nervously not knowing what to say as I glanced over at my friends. "What are you laughing at?" he said as he dug his nails deeper into my neck. I started to feel water forming underneath my eyes, but I held my tears back as best as I could. He then shoved me hard against the wall and walked off as I broke out in tears against his turned back, while my friends accompanied me to the principal's office.

Elementary school was rather difficult to go through. Sometimes, at lunch or after school when I was alone, that same little dark-skinned kid would come up to me and randomly hit me, whether I was just walking home or just peacefully playing basketball in the schoolyard. One time, a group of the little guy's friends circled me and called me names as I tried to break out of the circular prison they put me in. I acted as if the insults didn't affect me and walked out of the circle, tears trickling down my face as I dragged my feet across the schoolyard. My friends would ask what the problem was when they saw my sobbing, but I would just make up some random excuse because I didn't want to involve them in my problems.

It was a chilly Tuesday morning when I decided to head to school alone for the first time in my life. School was only of a couple blocks away, but it felt like a mile trek through Antarctica. As I was casually and slowly strolling to school, I spotted this skinny, dark-skinned male wearing a dark green zip-up hoodie and a black hat with the orange letters "Go Giants" on it. He looked as if he had just rolled down a mountain of dirt, with brown stains all over his clothing. As I approached the man, I started to look for potential escapes or ways to defend myself. I wondered how I would defend myself against a gun or a knife, or what I would do if he demanded money from me. I then snapped back into reality, slipped my hands into my warm pockets, and kept my eyes on the ground as I walked by, not daring to look up.

Throughout middle school, I completely avoided African Americans and just stayed completely within my own friend group. I tried to avoid communicating with them or just avoided them in general. I viewed them all as strong, fast, aggressive, and especially rude. I started putting all of them into the same category, not caring who they were, or where they came from. I never tried getting to know any of them, ending conversations short, or being completely awkward around them, not knowing what to say. I lived in fear around these people, thinking that they would hit me if I said the wrong thing or if I offended them.

Then high school came around. I had just transferred from my previous high school into Galileo and was placed into a course called Ethnic Studies. We went over many interesting topics, now that I look back on it, but at the time I found it a rather boring class. One time, we went over this topic called hegemony. I didn't really understand it at the time, but I knew it had something to do with stereotypes, or how our eyes weren't fully opened yet. Our Ethnic Studies teacher, Mr. Williams, kept comparing the topic to the movie *The Matrix,* and how we were like the people stuck in the capsules, living a dream without realizing that the lives we lived were all in our heads. To break through that dream, you had to wake up, like the main character Neo, and face reality.

I was sitting on a Muni bus just after a visit to the Westfield Mall after picking up a headset from Razer for $108 and buying some new clothes. I had the headset in a pink grocery bag along with the new clothes, and placed the bag between my feet. Then suddenly, as the bus came to a stop, a black man, probably in his forties or so, entered the bus. I instinctively sat straight up and pulled the bag up and held it close to my chest.

*Wait,* I thought. *Did I just assume that this random person who just got on the bus, probably headed for home just like I was, was going to steal from me?* I started to realize. The realization of judging someone before I even met them. The realization of what a horrible person I'd been all my life. The realization of making this person into someone he wasn't. The realization of what Mr. Williams had been talking about all along. It all came to me, in that very moment, and I felt ashamed.

This border that divided me from black people had finally been crossed. I started seeing the world differently, no longer was my mind instinctively assuming things about others. I started getting to know people without stereotypes getting in the way. I made new friends and started holding some enjoyable conversations. Looking back, I was just a timid, damaged little kid, believing everything people told me. Overall, I'm glad I took that Ethnic Studies class and had that enlightening moment. It helped me improve as a person and made me conscious of my absurd way of thinking.

And to conclude: Thank you, Mr. Williams.

---

*Peter C. is a fifteen-year-old student who attends Galileo High School. He was born in San Francisco in the year 2003. He enjoys playing basketball, listening to music, and playing video games. One day, he hopes to be able to create a video game of his own, one that he can be proud of and have people worldwide play the game! Additionally, he enjoys doing the mile run that his PE teacher makes him do every week.*

# GOODBYE DESPAIR

—

## KASSIE D.

This prestigious academy is the center of Tokyo city: Hope's Peak Academy. This academy gathers talented high school students from all over the world. There are only two steps to enroll. One: you have to be in high school. And two: you have to excel in your field. If you get accepted, you gain a title called an "Ultimate" to know what talent the school assigned you to.

Hope's Peak Academy is filled with amazing, talented, gifted students. So, how... how did I get accepted? Every time I walk inside the classroom everyone around me always asks the same question: "What is your talent?" To be honest, I have no idea. I don't know my talent or how I got accepted, but I never told my classmates the truth. I just change the topic whenever someone asks me. Everyone around me is so optimistic, so cheerful, and they all look so bright. When I'm around them I just feel like I'm in a dark void and it feels lonely. I've always wanted to go to this school, so why do I feel this way? Whatever.

I walked toward my desk and sat down. "Hey, Hajime!" *Here we go again.* A classmate ran toward me, bouncing up and down. "I know I keep on asking, but what's your talent?" As soon as she said that, many of my classmates gathered around, asking the same thing, as if it were a joke. I couldn't really respond to them, so I just giggled.

I'm not the only person at this school who doesn't have a talent. Every year, Hope's Peak has a lottery in which a student is chosen to attend even if they don't have a talent. The winner from my class is an athletic kid named Komaeda. However, Komaeda doesn't seem to mind his lack of talent. Instead, he takes out his insecurity by criticizing others.

Komaeda pushed through the crowd and made his way toward me. "Yeah, what is your talent? Don't you need one to go here?" he questioned. "I don't think being useless is a talent!" he laughed.

Everyone silently turned from Komaeda to me without making a sound. They weren't laughing at me, but it still felt like I was under a bright spotlight on stage.

"Ugh, whatever…" I mumbled as I gathered my things and walked away. I didn't want to show everyone how much Komaeda's words hurt me, because I still didn't feel like I belonged here. My friend Chiaki called out as she caught up to me.

"Hajime, wait!" I stopped and turned to her.

"What is it now? Are you going to ask me what my talent is too?" I said aggressively.

"No. You shouldn't listen to him. Or anyone else," she said calmly. "You're good at plenty of things! Like…" she drifted off into thought.

"Like what?" I interrupted in anger.

"Like helping people with their problems," Chiaki stated. "You always know what to say when things are difficult. Like when I felt alone during our first semester. I was stressed about my gaming test and you told me to just to be myself. You helped me a lot."

She wasn't wrong. I remember she was very stressed about her test. Chiaki was the best gamer in Hope's Peak and she needed to show the class she belonged there.

"But still, you're just saying that because you're my friend." I quietly said as I turned my back on her.

"No! I actually mean—"

"Chiaki, I don't need your pity, so leave me alone for now," I said as I walked away, eyes facing down.

The bell rang. I forgot I was supposed to stay in class. I turned around and Chiaki had already left. *Well, it's time to go back.* Time felt like it went by slower than before. Can this class be over already? A few more classes went by and school was over. I grabbed all my things and walked downstairs. When I was walking, I heard some loud chattering in a classroom. I slowly walked and went to open the door of the classroom where I heard loud chattering. As soon as I creaked the door open, I saw three students circling around an unexpected person, kneeling down and looking defenseless. Komaeda.

"You should know your place! You're acting so high and mighty as if you belong here! You're just here because of a stupid lottery. In the end you don't have talent at all!" A student yelled.

"..." Komaeda quietly slid his bag next to him and reached out a napkin from his bag. "Sorry that I spilled soda on yo—"

The student kicked Komaeda's bag, "You're sorry?" He let out a quick sigh and reached for his bag and took out a bottle of Coke. He unscrewed the cap. "Then I'll give you mine since you spilled your soda on me." Unexpectedly, he poured the soda on Komaeda. They all laughed, pointing at Komaeda. My eyes widened and I froze. They all walked toward the door and I quickly hid behind the corner of the wall. They were all laughing and high-fiving each other as they walked out of the classroom. I walked back to the classroom to check on Komaeda. He stood up and got his bag.

"Hey, are you okay?" I questioned.

"Why would you want to know?" He said, wiping his hair and clothes with a small tissue.

"Let's go to the water fountain," I hesitated.

"Ha, look, I don't need help." He pushed me aside to go through the door. As I saw him walk through the hallway, he slipped to the ground and quickly turned his head back at me, giving me a death stare. As much as I wanted to laugh, I decided to help him. I knew he didn't want any help, but I didn't like to see anyone in such a state.

Before I knew it, I was next to him washing his clothes as he was washing his hair in his PE uniform.

"Are you okay now?" I handed out a small towel.

"What's with you?" He snatched the towel from my hand and rubbed his head with it.

"Why? Is it not okay for me to be concerned?"

"Yes! Because a few hours ago I was just making fun of you. It's just weird."

"I know, but it just feels wrong to witness someone getting bullied. And I felt something familiar when they were hurting you," I said.

"Of course it felt familiar," he scoffed.

"No, I don't mean it that way. I mean I felt you're in a similar situation as me. Meaning that you felt hurt when they said you didn't belong here."

"You're saying that you're like me? No way," he said angrily.

"Yes, exactly. After all, you are here because of the lottery and I don't have a talent so I can see a connection." I saw him trembling as his face turned flaming red and he clenched his fist.

"No, we aren't alike at all! You're just a talentless nobody! And I have luck! I at least know I have a title, unlike you! If you think I don't have a talent it doesn't bother me at all, so don't act all friendly around me because you think we are alike," he roared.

"Stop lying to yourself. I saw you had the saddest look on your face when they told you that you don't have a talent," I said calmly as I straightened my back.

As he was about to open his mouth, I said, "I have a feeling that you also feel like you don't belong here even though you're a student, and that you feel lonely or angry that you don't even know your talent. So you take it out on other people by hurting them."

He sighed, but didn't say anything to stop me from talking. I could tell that he knew I was right. I clenched my left hand to my chest and continued to talk.

"Look. I know it feels horrible that you feel like you don't belong here. But at least you have something you're good at…" I placed my hand on my chin. "Making people feel entertained! You make people laugh. I know you make people laugh in a bad way, but at least you have something." I clasped my hands together, hoping that he would feel a bit better. I could tell by reading his facial expression that he wasn't believing me at all. *Come on, think of a time that he's done something good. Oh!*

"I remember you in the debate club! I saw you when I was passing by and you were amazing! Your claims and evidence were so clear! Even though it was about a fake murder case, you were able to figure out everything!" I said cheerfully.

"Really? I did pretty horribly and we didn't even win."

"It didn't matter if you won or not, you were great!"

"I guess so…" he said. I could tell that he was trying to hold back his smile. He continuously rubbed his hair with the towel. Then he threw it on my face and turned around.

"Maybe you aren't useless after all," he murmured. After he said that, he walked out of the school gates and disappeared from my sight. I didn't understand what he meant by that, but I smiled.

The next day at school, I noticed things had changed. Komaeda wasn't bothering me. Actually, no one was bothering me. I stopped hearing the same questions over and over again. During the entire class I was confused, yet relieved. Lunch came by and so did Chiaki. She leaned toward me with her gleaming eyes

"What just happened? How did you do it?"

I furrowed my brow in confusion and said, "Huh, what do you mean?"

As I drank my water, she leaned away from me and gave me space.

"You know Komaeda, right? He said that he would stop bothering you and said you have a talent. I heard him saying that to a couple of our classmates who were confused about how he wasn't making fun of you."

I spit out my drink leaving a mess on the table. "Wait, what? The dude that has been bullying me my whole high school life, just because I have no talent, said that I have a talent? Yeah, right."

Chiaki noticed that I didn't believe her at all. She sat down and clasped her hands on the table. "Did you know what talent he said you had?" A small pause came and I waited for the answer. She sighed and smiled.

"It's okay if you don't know. I'll let you figure that out. You may be blind to it right now, but it's clear to me and him that you have something."

"What? You're going to leave me with a cliffhanger?! Just tell me!" I whined.

She stood up and said, "I'll give you a hint."

"What is it? What is it?"

"I already told you a long time ago, so think back about it."

She walked away, waving me goodbye as she smiled. *How am I supposed to remember what she said? I can't even remember what I ate for breakfast! UGH.* I thought as long and hard as I could. Throughout the day, during class I was distracted thinking about what she said. Even walking home, I was thinking about it. I went inside my house, showered, changed my clothes, ate dinner, and went straight to bed. I laid down with my eyes closed. Time went by. *Ah, I remember now.*

---

**Kassie D.** *was born in San Francisco and is fifteen years old. She likes to draw and make video edits. She does cheerleading for sports and enjoys playing volleyball. In the future, she would like to make a comic book. She has two dogs, a Pit Bull mix and a Great Dane.*

# RETROSPECT

—

## KEVIN G.

**H**ave you ever thought about how racism can affect others? It doesn't just affect their feelings, but it can create fear for their safety. How do I know this? I've been through these experiences. I've been there, and I have also seen it. It is not just me, it's the whole world that can be affected, like a virus. I was nine years old when I became aware of this issue.

My father and I were walking down the street after we got our hair cut. We had parked just a few blocks away. The street smelled like food fused with the faint smell of smoke. The sky was gray and it was not the best day, either. It was an ordinary day, but I suspected that something sinister was going to occur. I felt like my chest was warning me. My dad and I stopped into this sketchy corner store.

The outside of it had stickers and graffiti all over it. We went in and it was dirty just like a regular corner store, but more dirty than you usually expect, and smelled like a bunch of cigarettes. We walked by the counter, and we saw a person who we suspected was the shop owner. He was Asian, short (he needed a stool to reach the counter), and elderly-looking (there was barely any black hair on his head). He kept a real close eye on us like we were up to something. We went to the chips area, then we noticed the ceiling—it was a bunch of mirrors. We saw our reflection and right after, we noticed even more reflections of ourselves.

So many mirrors placed on the wall to the point where the shop owner could see every single angle. An African American man appeared just a few seconds after we found out about the mirrors. He looked a little over six feet tall, big and strong. So strong you could see his veins popping out. Then suddenly, the shop owner got scared and he pulled out a gun. I put my hands right up and dropped everything that I had in my hands.

I was so terrified. I couldn't think straight. It was as if my soul had left my body. Pointing the gun between the African American man, my dad, and me, he yelled, "Try to steal something and I will shoot. This won't happen again." I did not know how to feel at that point. I stood there for seconds that felt like hours. I still had my arms up. Then my dad grabbed my hands to try and put them down slowly, with caution, while the shop owner still had the gun out. We walked slowly with our hands where the shop owner could see them while he was aiming the weapon toward us.

It was like I was in a movie. A bad one. Moving slowly, hearing an echo of my dad's voice, my body felt cold. My smile was gone. Time just stopped. We walked away with nothing but fear. I was breathing heavily and fast like I had just run a marathon.

But that day I realized there was a bigger problem in this neighborhood, this city, this state, this country. This world. It felt angry, with no smiles and no happiness. I had to take a few days to process what had just happened. The fact that a gun was brought out and was pointed directly toward me was even more terrifying. That feeling never left right away. It stayed with me for such a long time. That moment the guy pulled out the weapon. I could've died. I could've lost my dad that day, too. A life could have been lost. In the years that I have been living in this world, I have lost family members. Close and far away, but it still affected me. I lost a family member because of racism. He and his brother were shot, but unfortunately, only his brother lived. And it was all because of their race. It was a white guy who fired a gun at them, although I know not everyone is the same. He had reasons for why to shoot. I can't imagine the pain of seeing your sibling lying next to you. Lifeless. Without a heartbeat, while you were suffering the same pain as them. It makes me anxious whenever I go places alone. Different people have different perspectives about why they do what they do. Have you ever felt this way before?

Have you ever thought about how racism can affect you and others?

------------

*Kevin G. was born and raised in San Francisco. He is fifteen years old. He enjoys listening to music as much as he enjoys drawing. He also likes playing sports and if you treat him right, he'll treat you right.*

# WINDOWS AND DOORS
—

## DANIELA G.

I became aware of it when I asked my parents during middle school if I could go out, and every time I would ask, they would say no. They were so strict with me. They never let me go anywhere, by myself or with my friends. It felt like I was being held hostage. I would ask them why, and they would always make up the same excuse: that I'm not going to be careful and that I need to put in effort from my side, and by this they meant I needed to get good grades and only focus on school. I was trying really hard in all my classes, with Bs and Cs, but they wanted all As. I became tired of them always saying something negative to me, telling me my grades weren't good, or them just not being pleased with what I got.

They would only let me go out once in a month or even less. When I did go out, they would call me every time, asking where I'm at, and they always got mad at me for not answering my phone. This would lead to arguments and them telling me I'm disrespectful when I talk back. So, I ended up not talking back, yet they still said it's disrespectful for ignoring them, which led to even longer times of me not going out. My friends would always ask me to go out with them, but sometimes I wouldn't even bother to ask my parents for permission, since they rarely even let me out. I usually just go home after school, or maybe to practice, but other than that I would never go anywhere or go explore and have fun with my friends.

I got so frustrated I began to skip classes. I'd skip a few classes with Amalia. We would go eat or just hang out and talk. One Wednesday, we decided to skip and go to get pizza on North Point St. and Hyde. I got a pepperoni pizza with mushrooms, and she got a regular pepperoni pizza with a side of ranch. We went to Ghirardelli Square to go sit and eat. When we got there, we saw tourists roaming around talking in their own native languages and admiring the buildings. We sat near the ping pong table and talked about what's been going on at school, for example rumors we've heard. It felt great to not go to class and be stuck in a room for forty minutes or more. When I got home, my dad came straight to my room and asked me why he had gotten a phone call from the school. I gave him an excuse that I wasn't feeling good and that I went to wellness center.

Even though I was really happy and free when I was cutting, I began to notice how skipping class wasn't doing me any good. After I had cut school maybe six times, I started to notice that my grades were dropping. I now had some Ds and my chemistry grade went down to an F. I wasn't proud at all. It felt like I was thinking exactly the same things that my parents were thinking: I wasn't trying. I wasn't even showing up to class. I was feeling down, but this time it was not from them, it was from me. So, I decided to change, and not for them, but for me. When the new semester started, I stopped skipping class, I did all my homework (especially in Chemistry), and I began to study my teachers' "Do Nows" that were written on the board at the start of class.

This is also when I began to see where my parents were coming from. They both wanted me to do really well in school because they didn't have the same opportunities for education I have since they came from Guatemala and Mexico. I guess they want me to live the American Dream, but they have a weird way of showing it. They try to motivate me in their own way, which isn't the best way. They never say good job or show that they are proud of me, even though I wish they would. They believe they have to be strict and negative to motivate me. They want me to have a better life than they have, and want me to be a role model for my little brother. They just don't know the words to use. But I changed my own perspective, changed the negative things they have to say into a better way of seeing it. Even if they don't appreciate what I do in school, I don't listen to their negative opinions. I believe in myself and know my own worth.

When I would ask my parents if I could go out with friends, I would feel and still do feel, nervous because I'm so used to them saying no. One afternoon, I came home and noticed my parents were in the living room with my brother watching TV, with my dog running around, birds chirping, and the smell of plants. I closed the front door and sat down next to my mom. I whispered to her, asking if I could go out on Wednesday to go ice skating with Leslie. She said, "I don't know. Ask your dad." And he asked my mom what I told her. He asked what time I would leave the house and what time I would come back. I asked if that meant a yes, because why ask me and not let me go out? He said he would think about it, and he always says this when I ask him something, which leads to him saying no.

Later that day he came into my room. He heard music blasting while I was doing homework, I most likely think it was Kodak Black playing at the time. He then told me to turn it down and gave me permission to go ice skating with my friend. Turns out it was a happy ending for me that day.

———

*Daniela G.* *was born in Mexico and is fifteen years old. She has a brother who is younger than she is. She loves dogs and the color blue. She plans on going to a four-year college.*

# THE CALL
—

## JESUS G.

One late night when I got home from a friend's house, I went onto my bed, and since it was a weekend, I was chillin' on my phone going through Snap stories, replying to some people. Then about an hour or two later of me being on my phone, my mom eventually received a phone call from a local jail, which turned out to be my sister. Since my mother had her phone on speaker, I was able to eavesdrop. I heard her crying saying, *"Estoy... estoy en la cárcel, Ma,"* and my mom, crying, replied with, *"¿Porque estás en la cárcel?"*

After that, I couldn't hear any dialogue. It just fell silent in our room while my brother and I tried listening in on their conversation about what happened, but we couldn't hear anything. It just felt like no one was in the room anymore. We all heard a loud ring, meaning the call was about to end, then we heard, *"No te preocupes. Todo esta bien."* Then, the call ended. After their talk, we all heard my mom talking to my stepdad, saying that her bail was $30,000. Once we all heard that, the room fell silent. Then, the room that always felt like joy and warmth turned into a room that felt cold and sad. Throughout the rest of that day, everyone was just silent. No one said anything to anyone until eventually everyone fell asleep. One by one phones were being turned off. Finally, it was only me and my brother awake and by this time it was already 4:00 a.m. When he went to sleep, his last words before he did were, "Tomorrow will be a better day...now go to sleep." I replied back with "Goodnight." But of course, I didn't...it was about 6:00 a.m. then. My stepdad woke up to get ready for work, which meant I should probably go sleep and I did for eight full hours.

It was about two something in the afternoon. I started that day like I always do, by doing my chores, but when I finished, I didn't really do anything afterward. I would've usually hung out with friends, but instead I just sat there as if I were paralyzed. Eventually, I was checked in on, to see if I was okay.

## "Then, the room that always felt like joy and warmth turned into a room that felt cold and sad."

"Yeah, I'm fine," I said, actually thinking if I was or wasn't okay. Eventually, the phone rang, and we thought it was going to be a call from work, but it turned out it was a call from the jail my sister was in. How the rest of us found out was by the, "This is a prepaid call from __. To accept this call, please press 0. To decline, press 5." Since we were a noisy bunch, we couldn't really hear anything they were saying. All we heard was my mom saying, *"¿Estás bien?"* followed by tears. A minute passed. Then all we heard from our room was a bunch of noise, as if we were packing. So being the nosy person I am, I went into the other room to see what she was doing. Once I went through that door, all I saw was a mess of things all over the room. Eventually, I asked my mom what she was looking for and she said, *"Estoy buscando un papel para ayudar a tu hermana."*

*"¿Cual tipo de papel estás buscando?"* I asked.

*"Un papel del abogado,"* she replied.

"Oh."

That's the only thing I could think of to say because my train of thought went somewhere else, as if I wasn't able to understand what she was saying. Eventually, she found the lawyer's card. She gave him a call and told him about our situation.

It was two weeks since we had heard from my sister and it was a Friday afternoon. My oldest brother was at work, my stepbrother was at a *quince* practice, my mom's boyfriend and my youngest brother had gone to Oakland, so then it was only me and my mom. I finished my chores and it was about 4:00 p.m. I wanted to leave the house, but everyone I hung out with was either home or hanging with other people. Eventually, I got bored so I started to sketch while I was blasting music. It was about 6:00 p.m. and I still wasn't done. Then out of nowhere, I started missing my sister. I started remembering memories of when we were younger. She is older than I am by seven years. Then I found a picture book my sister kept in her stuff. I looked through it and thought about how much we all had changed, how much we had grown. I saw a photo of when she held me when I was younger. My sister is the type of person that will tell you the truth even if it was hard. She would tell me and my brother almost everything. She would give us advice about things randomly. While I was in the middle of the book, I heard my name being called from the other room.

"Andres."

I went to the room to see my mom on the phone with someone. Not knowing who it was, I went to the other room to keep sketching. Then I got called back in.

*"Andy, ven para aca,"* my mom said.

*"¿Que quieres?"* I asked.

*"Marca este dia,"* she said.

*"¿Qual dia?"* I asked.

"*El 28 de este mes,*" Mom answered.

"*¿Por qué?*"

"*Es el día que podemos mira tu hermana en la corte. Yo no puedo ir porque no tengo papeles.*"

"*¿Y yo puedo ir?*" I asked.

"*Vas a ir con tu padrastro,*" Mom said.

I answered, "*Okay, pues.*"

It was about two weeks, right before the court date on a Tuesday night, when someone knocked on the door at 1:00 a.m. We opened the door to see it was my sister standing there, crying. We let her in and we asked her how she got out. The only thing she told us was, "He confessed everything…and they let me out." We didn't go the next day to court because no one said anything about my sister's boyfriend's court date.

———————

*Jesus G. was born in Selma, California and was raised in the Tenderloin. He likes to draw and listen to music. He works at a restaurant with his two brothers and sister.*

# THE ROCK

—

**ZARIE H.**

One day, I was exploring the village forest when I finally came across the rock. This rock was a border for the people of my village. The rock was almost completely covered in moss. While examining it, I saw some engraved words on it. It was written in a language long forgotten in the village. The only records of this language existing were on this rock. I had always wondered what could be found beyond it, as did others before me. Legend has it that those who went beyond it never came back. Some think it's because they died. Others think it is because whatever is beyond it is so beautiful no one would ever want to leave. The rock had been here since my people found this land.

When my generation arrived here, the rock was nowhere in sight, and the leader at the time was Zam. He was said to be the best leader there'd ever been. There was a drawing of him in the middle of the village. He was tall, about 6'3", with black hair and a red and green talisman around his neck. That same talisman was displayed in the museum of old artifacts. He had spoken the old language and was rumored to be a spell caster. Many of the people at the time had tried their best to pick up on the language, but no one could fully understand it. Some think he was the one who engraved the words onto the rock and enabled the barrier. When his three children turned ten years old, it is said that he disappeared and was never seen again. That was 200 years ago.

Looking past the rock, I wondered if I should continue my journey and walk past it, or throw my curiosity to the side and go back home. Ever since I was young, I wanted to explore and go on adventures. I would never pass up an opportunity to see something new. Once I turned twenty, I thought I'd seen everything possible and explored every inch of land I could.

The current leader, San, had announced a couple weeks ago that we were running low on resources and to get them we needed access to places beyond the village. People were starting to starve because of the lack of plants and animals within the barrier, and despite their best efforts, the villagers couldn't get out. After the announcements, while walking back home, I heard a story one of the elders was telling. The story was about a man of royal descent that would save the village and break the barrier. After hearing the story, it dawned upon me that I could be the hero that saved the village and possibly bring back the leader. Unknowing if I was of royal blood or not, I was willing to try it for my people.

It was a cold, cloudy night and there was a full moon. It was orangish. Before leaving on my journey, I snuck into the museum of old artifacts, dodging security and soldiers, and took the talisman with me, just in case. Looking back on my village for what seemed like the last time, I thought about my family. Then I took a deep breath and took the first step past the rock. I fell into a darkness blacker than night.

I woke up to a beautiful sunrise and birds chirping. It seemed as if I hadn't moved past the rock, until I turned around to look back at my village and was greeted by a frightening sight. It was in ruins with vines around the stones, and there wasn't much left of the trees that once reached to the heavens. There was no one in sight. It seemed as if it had been abandoned for years. *But that couldn't be, everyone was just here and everything should be the same.* Then I thought to myself, *how long have I been out for?* I pulled out my knife so that I could see my reflection on it. I still looked the same. Then it came to me: *what if the stories that the village people told were true, and I'd been transported to another dimension?* I looked back at the spot that was once my home. There was nothing left, not even the blocks of stone that once structured it. The rock that once kept everyone in with its barrier was now inactive. With nothing left and no one in sight, I started walking. I finally got farther beyond the rock. I was always curious about the rock and going this far beyond it was something that many people including myself thought was impossible. I didn't know what to do or where to go, so I kept walking.

After walking for what seemed to be forever, I came across a weird machine. It had four big wheels on it and windows. I looked closer and saw a silhouette of a person, then I started to run toward it. Once I reached it, I started inspecting it even more, when a voice came from inside saying, "Get away from my truck, you weirdo." The man got out with a club in his hand and ran toward me. I tried to tell him I wasn't trying to hurt him or his truck. With every word he said, the language sounded even more familiar, as if I had heard it before. When I was finally able to put my finger on it, I realized that this man was speaking the old language that was once spoken by the eldest leader, Zam. Once I opened my mouth and tried to talk, the talisman started to glow, and all of a sudden, I was able to understand him and speak the language as well as he did. After he stopped yelling, I asked him if he knew anything about a man named Zam. I described him to the man and he told me that he had a grandfather named Zam, but my description was a little off. Looking confused, he asked if I knew him or not.

I quietly said, "Please bring me to him. We must talk." Still looking confused, he told me to hop into the truck. I said thank you and got inside the truck. On the way there, we talked and he told me his name was James. He asked me where I was from and if I lived close to there. I told him about the village and how when I had woken up, everything had been gone.

He said, "Village, huh? No wonder you're wearing those weird clothes." He told me that we were getting close and we would be there in a short while. I looked and, in the distance, I saw a giant house. It looked like it was inspired by the ones in the village. We pulled up to a big, shiny gate with a lot of what seemed to be security around it.

"What are those things the men are holding?" I asked. He told me that they were guns and they were very lethal. The gates were made of gold and were diamond encrusted. I asked James why Zam had all the security. All he told me was that Zam was a very famous man that needed security so his property wasn't defaced. After passing through the gates, we drove up to the home and got out to start walking up the many steps that led to the front door. Many things around Zam's home reminded me of mine. It smelled similar to how it did in the village. All this evidence led me to believe that this had to be the long-lost leader I was looking for. When we finally reached the door, James rang the bell. Upon inspecting it, I saw the mark on his door was the same as the one that was engraved into the rock.

A man opened the door, but it wasn't him. James asked the man, "Where is my grandfather?"

He responded, "He is working in his study, but who is this man that you have brought along with you?"

This time I wanted to respond, but I was too fascinated with the talisman's glow, so James answered again with, "He is just a relative."

So, the man took us up to the study where Zam was. I was so shocked that I would finally be able to see him in person. He looked the same as his picture in the village. He took one glance at me and noticed the clothing and talisman. He looked shocked to see one of his descendants. He told me that he already knew why I was here and that he could help me. He told me that when the tribe first arrived to the spot where the village was now, there were a lot of dangerous things there, so he put a spell on the rock that could only be broken by someone that had spoken his language. The catch was only his family would be able to exit the barrier to find him. After telling me the story, he gave me a piece of paper with some words on it I could barely read. He read it out loud slowly. He told me that if I spoke this spell near the rock that I would be able to go back home. Then on the back of the paper he wrote something else and spoke it aloud for me to hear. He said, "When you get back home, go to the rock and say this and the barrier will break." He told me that it was great to see me and to tell the people of the village that he loved them. So, I took the spells and told James to take me back to the place he found me.

On the way back, James asked me what happened in the study. I told him about the village and the problem we had. He nodded and said, "Okay." We finally reached the spot and I thanked James for what he had done for me. I closed his door and started sprinting toward the village ruins. By the time I reached them it was very dark. I saw the rock and spoke the spell that Zam had given me. The rock split in half and a portal-like thing opened up. Before stepping through it, I took one more glance at the old ruins then said, "I won't let this happen." Then, I stepped through.

When I stepped through, I woke up and all the village people stood around me. It was morning now. The guards grabbed me and said I was under arrest for stealing the talisman, but before they grabbed me, I told them that I met Zam and he told me how I could break the barrier. None of the village people believed me, so I spoke the words from the back of the paper out loud, and the engraved words on the rock turned blue. I told them it was safe to pass it now. Most still didn't believe, but those who did started to walk past it one by one, until almost all the villagers were out. They all cheered for me and said that I had saved them, and the barrier was finally broken.

---

*Zarie H. was born and raised in San Francisco. He is sixteen years old. He likes to play video games and listen to music. He also likes to play football. When he graduates, he hopes to go to college and study to become a lawyer.*

# LEAVING A PART OF ME BEHIND

—

**CALLY H.**

It was a Monday morning just like any other day. I was walking down my middle school hall wearing my gray jacket and my everyday Free Runs. Everyone made their way to class, leaving me with a guy and a girl on our way to class. As I was walking to my math class, thinking about what I should do after school, suddenly this tall guy trips me and I fall with my textbook and notebooks scattering all over the floor. He didn't look to see if I was fine or help me up. He just said, "My bad," and walked away. From a distance, I heard the girl that was walking to the same class ask me if I was okay. I didn't reply to her because all I was thinking about was that I fell, and my knees hurt. I felt embarrassed. In my head I wanted to yell at the guy for not caring. If I had yelled, I would have felt relieved or forgiven him. I wanted to speak up, but I didn't because I just couldn't get the words out of my mouth. It was as if the thoughts in my head were piling up behind a wall, a wall of fear of being judged by others. Like I'm trying to speak up, but it's blocking me from speaking up. It was as if my words were trying to get into a stranger's house. You knock on the door, but no one is opening the door.

To me, a border is the fear of being judged by others. To cross this border, you need to be confident and forget what others think of you. I became aware of this border when I was in middle school. I realized most of my classmates said what was on their minds. They didn't really care about what others thought about them. Not speaking up for myself made me feel like an outsider, like no one wanted to talk to me or be friends with me. I was a quiet girl in middle school. A lot of my classmates always asked me, "Why are you so quiet?" I've always said what I wanted to say, but only in my mind. When I speak up for myself, I feel more confident. The line to that border starts to fade a little.

When I was three years old, my mom would bring me to the park. She would tell me that whenever a kid would come up to me to play, I would start crying. When I started elementary school, I would cry a lot in kindergarten. Mostly every day in the beginning of kindergarten I would go to the office and say I was sick just so I could go home and not be at school with people I didn't know. After being comfortable with everyone, I became loud and said what was on my mind. But whenever we had school plays, I would get anxious and overthink everything.

"To me, a border is the fear of being judged by others. To cross this border, you need to be confident, and forget what others think of you."

As time passed, I graduated elementary school and moved on to middle school. I guess I already had the shyness in me as a kid. When I started middle school, I didn't know that many people, I didn't talk as much or try to make any friends like I did in elementary school. More time passed, and that shyness started to come out of me and became a part of me, like a jacket that's been in my closet for years that I never wore and decided to wear again. In middle school when people would try to start a conversation with me, I would answer their questions and look away. I wouldn't talk to them for more time than I absolutely had to. In my head I wanted to start a conversation by saying, "What did you do in your previous period?" or "What are your plans this weekend?" Back then I didn't know how to start conversations with other people. I would just sit at my table quietly and listen to my classmates talk.

When I was in middle school, I didn't talk much to other students. Other students didn't talk to me because they might have thought that I was shy and innocent. I'm Asian so people make assumptions about me that I'm quiet, smart, or I don't cuss. When I cussed in class my classmate said, "Cally, I didn't know you cuss." When I am with my friends I am comfortable, but when I meet new people there is still that shyness in me. It takes a while for me to open up when I meet new people. Now that I've spent a few years with my friends, they tell me that they thought I was nice and quiet, but as they got to know me, they say I'm a lot more social and talkative.

During high school my older sister was also in the same school as me. I hung out with her and her friends. When we stood in a circle and had conversations, I'd step back. My sister would pull me back in and tell me, "You should talk, too." At that moment it made me even more nervous.

At home when I was alone with my mom, she would ask me if I participated in class or made any new friends. I'd tell her that I was afraid to make new friends and talk at school. My mom said to me, "You don't need to care about what people think of you. You do whatever you're doing and be confident in yourself."

I started to take my older sister and mom's advice. I learned to overcome the fear of speaking up. I can express my feelings and say what's on my mind more. There may also be others who feel like an outsider who are afraid to speak up, and that's not something people should put themselves down for. When I was in middle school, I would put myself down because I was introverted. I would tell myself that no one wanted to be friends with me, and that I should just be by myself because I didn't fit in. I started to believe the words I told myself. Believing the words that I told myself would lead me to think that no one wanted to talk to me because I was quiet and shy, and that led me to have glossophobia. I felt like whenever I was in public, I would speak softly, and I felt like everyone was staring at me. When I got to high school, I realized that I felt like no one came up to me because I didn't try to open up and talk to them. A lot of my classmates talked a lot. They wouldn't sit by themselves in class like I used to. So, I decided to change the way I thought of myself. I'd try to start conversations, ask questions, and make friends. Now I've made more friends and learned to start conversations. I try to speak up as much as I can when I speak in public. You shouldn't be afraid to speak up for what you want, because when I was silent it meant yes to other people. But if you're afraid, one day you will learn to conquer your fear and cross that border.

---

*Cally H. was born in California. She currently attends Galileo High School. She likes to do arts and crafts and hang out with her friends or siblings during her free time. Her goals are to get into a UC and travel the world.*

# IN BETWEEN

—

## JOANNE H.

A kaleidoscope of lotus flowers
blanket a pond under
an intricately carved stone bridge.

Eating out of bowls instead of plates,
fragrant ribs in a new Hong Kong crib.

ACs were blowing a cool breeze,
but this trip was no breeze at all.

Smog like an oven
constantly smothers buildings
with an ugly, pungent stench.

As I leaned back in my chair,
I could feel my sweat-soaked t-shirt
stick to me like sweet honey boba

Noises everywhere,
car horns blaring,
shopkeepers yelling like it's Black Friday.

Indecipherable "scribbles"
of the Chinese language
everywhere
I turn.

Back in the Bay Area,
windy breeze blows through
plentiful dandelions.

Clear blue skies like cut glass,
warm sunshine breaks through like a prism.

A rainbow of new languages and people on familiar buses
from North Beach
to Castro.

Back in their homeland,
under the shared umbrella,
humid, pouring rain led
my dad to snuggle my mom affectionately.

Something I'd never seen.

While me, fooled
by McD's familiar Golden Arches,
uncomfortable doing something that was simple back home,
I looked back at my dad with pleading eyes,
urging him to help me;
dumbfounded
the unfamiliar burger was not enjoyable.

Camouflaged by a sea of Chinese people,
but unable to break their spoken code.

Back at home,
my mom asks me to read the mail again,
a page full of unreadable scribbles to her;
I understand it, but with my limited vocabulary,
I can't explain it.

Having to ask what my parents want
at the Starbucks counter,
I am often embarrassed to speak in a foreign language;
I can feel those waiting behind me start to get impatient,
judging me.

When we're away,
we may both miss our homelands,
but home is wherever we are
together.

Having dealt with language borders my whole life,
it isn't a big struggle nor is it easygoing; more just
in between.

---

*Joanne H. was born in San Francisco and is sixteen years old. She loves to read books and play sports like tennis and badminton. Her favorite way to pass time is to watch shows. In the future, she'd like to get a good job so that she could live comfortably. She is considering something maybe in the medicine department. She also loves golden retrievers.*

# MY DREAM JOB
—

## ROMAISSA K.

When I was a little girl of four or five, I always dreamed of being a police officer. I always thought it would be a fun thing to do because it also included saving people, which was my favorite part. I've always had this idea growing up.

Every time I talked to my parents about it, they just laughed and said, "You know, we all think that you should be a doctor, honey, or a dentist instead..." I didn't like that idea or the way they tried to change the subject. I used to argue with them about it. I felt like they were picking my dream job or career for me. When I was about ten years old, my father kept telling me that being a police officer could be very dangerous. Back in my country, men were the ones who made all necessary decisions for women, in every situation, no matter what. But I always hated that and wanted to stand up for myself and do what I felt was right for me, without disrespecting my parents. I always knew that being a police officer would be a very inspiring job to do.

My mom is a doctor. She was raised in a family of five and she was the only daughter and also the most loved one. As she told me, her parents were also very strict about a lot of things. She wasn't allowed to do a lot of things that she wanted to do, but she was still able to follow her dream and she made her way through.

One day, I was very mad because of what my father was telling me about how I was supposed to be a doctor, and my mother just sat me down and told me, "Romaissa, we all know this is a dangerous job (or at least your father thinks that), but you can make your way through just like I did. I believe in you and I'm sure you can convince him when it's time. You've just got to be very patient." I took her words very seriously, and by doing that, I learned how to be patient.

My mother was supporting my dad, obviously, because that was her job as a married woman, so she didn't really have the right to decide, but she always told me that even if she didn't say, "Let her be whatever she wants," to my dad, she still wanted to say it. She was a great woman with a big heart. She loved everyone. She was tall with tan skin and curly hair that I used to love to play with.

I have a great uncle and his name is Ahmed. He is tall and very strong. He is about 6'4" with dark black hair and brown eyes. Uncle Ahmed, who I call Dede, lived with me and my parents growing up. He was my favorite one in the house. He was a police officer—a great officer for ten years in France. He had a really soft voice and heart. Uncle Dede got shot in Paris, France during a robbery. That made his life very difficult. He stayed in the hospital for about two months. His wife, who I call Tata, would visit him in the hospital every day and sometimes even sleep there. Since we were all the way in Algeria and couldn't go to France, we were very worried, especially my grandma. She used to cry all the time and she wished she could go and see him, but she wasn't able to until he was out of the hospital.

I remember when I was little and he used to live with us. He would carry me on his back and run all over the house just for fun. When my grandma would tell us to stop playing around, he told me to ignore her because she wasn't fun like us. One time, he came to visit over the summer and he brought his police uniform: his belt, his badge…I was about eight years old at that time. I loved his stuff and I kept trying on his uniform. His uniform and badge made me think I wanted to be a police officer. After what happened to him, my father got even more serious about his opposition to me being a police officer. Every time I talked about it, he said, "Don't you remember what happened to your uncle? And you still want to be a police officer? You're out of your mind." I eventually got tired of all the conversations and arguments I used to have with him. But I always had nice conversations with Dede.

# "I always knew that being a police officer would be a very inspiring job to do."

One day, he was telling me about this time when he was working and caught two people stealing, and I found that story very funny and made him repeat it to me every time I saw him.

"Dede, have you ever gone undercover?" He told me stories about chasing thieves and going undercover.

"Yes, all the time. One day, me and my partner had to go undercover for a whole week and we had to act like we were part of this group just to take them down because they were doing illegal things, and we finally took them down."

I kept asking him questions about the story until I knew all the details and he got tired of me. He told me many stories that I loved. What happened to him in France was a very bad thing. I couldn't accept the incident and was shook.

After I moved to San Francisco, I stopped talking to my father about being a police officer for about three years. When I mentioned it again, I felt like he changed a little bit.

"Daddy, I think I still want to be a police officer. It has been always my favorite job…"

"Do you think you'd really love to be a police officer?"

"Yes, I just want to follow my dream and do this job without disrespecting you and Mommy."

"I would say you should think about it again, but if you don't want to, it's all your decision…"

I kept wondering what happened to him. Why did he change his mind? Then, I thought of how he hadn't seen me in six years. Maybe he just doesn't want me to be sad and he wants me to do what I think is right for myself.

———

*Romaissa K.* *was born in Algeria and is now sixteen. She loves to play soccer, listen to music, and watch football. She loves spicy food a lot and dreams to be a doctor, a teacher, or a police officer.*

# THE BERKELEY DREAM

—

## CHRIS L.

**I never realized** money would be a border I had to cross to follow my goals. One day, my math teacher asked the class what college we wanted to go to. In my mind, I wanted to go to Berkeley, but I was too shy to answer. All of a sudden, the class was in chaos, as students yelled out colleges left and right. The sound of kids yelling could be heard by classes next door. I thought it would never end until the teacher told us to quiet down. He chuckled and told us to say it one at a time. So, one at a time, each student yelled out colleges they wanted to go to. Most of the colleges were well-known and close. UC Berkeley came up the most, so we used that school as an example. He told us about expenses for that school, such as tuitions and fees. I never knew the cost of attending Berkeley and this was the first time I had noticed this border. I wondered how I would be able to afford attending Berkeley.

My family settled in San Francisco twenty years ago and they wish they had gone to a university, especially Berkeley. I guess that stuck with them because I was constantly reminded to go to Berkeley at home. I started to have second thoughts about Berkeley, but the thought of disappointing my family was tough. I was trapped in a seemingly endless cycle and I had no clue how to get out. I was lost.

I've thought about this for a long time and every time I think about it, I start to realize how much this border affects me. A few months ago,

I went on a tour to Berkeley and I realized they have the best computer science program in the country. I really wanted to pursue computer programming as a career, but it seemed less and less possible. I would imagine myself as a student in Berkeley and how I'd be able to pursue my goals, but it was all just a dream. I knew this might not be a permanent border, but it'll be a miracle to cross this invisible border preventing me from doing what I want to do.

During class one day, I asked my friend what college he wants to go to and he told me a small college near where he lives. I had a feeling I knew why he decided to pick that college, but I didn't want to ask. I knew he didn't want to go to a small college because he believed small colleges wouldn't be good enough for him. This border was not only affecting me, but him as well. I knew I wasn't alone anymore. I never really noticed borders are a part of everyone's life until now. Countless borders prevent me from doing something, and money is just one of them. It may not be easy to cross this border, but I, as well as many others, will have to eventually.

———————

*Chris L. was born in California. He is fifteen years old. He loves computer programming. His plans for the future include becoming a software engineer. He likes to create.*

# TAKING THAT EXTRA STEP

—

## SALLY L.

Hi, my name is Sally and I'm an only child. I like to part my hair in the middle. When I was a little kid, I daydreamed of having an Xbox. Now I like to be alone in my room and play video games all day. But I regret not being productive when I have the time to do so. I regret a lot of things. I'm scared of a lot of things. The first time I remember feeling fear was when I tried talking to new people. This is probably why I never go out. I don't really belong in a group. I don't really fit in.

That fear of speaking and talking to other people just stuck with me as I grew older. A lot of things go through my mind when I'm having a conversation with someone. *Should I say this? Oh no, what if I say something wrong? Are they going to think I'm weird after this?* I say to myself. It's almost like there are two different voices in my head. I want the confidence to speak up in front of a class or to my friends at school. I want to be able to say what's on my mind at that moment in time, especially when I'm with my friends. I want to feel comfortable.

One day, I'm walking into class and I sit down in my seat. I look around and I'm in the clear. All of a sudden, Nick enters the room and is headed straight toward me. He begins to speak. He talks to me like a police officer interrogating a criminal. "So, who does Anahi like?" he asks. My heart races. My palms begin to sweat. I start to become anxious. Anahi told me who she liked and the word spread out that I knew who it was. I'm really close with Anahi and I want her to trust me, but I also don't want to betray the trust of Nick. My head starts spinning. *If I tell Nick, what if he tells someone else? If I don't say anything about Nick talking to me, will Anahi think I'm hiding something?* I begin to speak.

A few months have passed. I just got my new Nike Elite backpack. I'm swaggering down the halls listening to my R&B music with my Beats headphones. My backpack is slightly sagged down. I can hear the sound of my pencils bouncing around. As I walk into math class, I hear my friend Kevin by the door speaking like a sports announcer, "Ladies and gentlemen, standing at 5′2″ with a career high of *two* points, here comes SALLY L.!" I smile and nudge him a little as I walk into the classroom and hear my friends laughing at me.

I was filled with embarrassment and humiliation, but I felt happy as well. I felt like a basketball player subbing into their first game: nervous, but as they played, they hear their friends cheering for them on the bleachers, taking away their fear. I walked into class and wasn't worried about what people thought of me or what people said about me, even if I only scored two points out of all the games in the season.

As the school year goes by, I begin to feel more and more comfortable when speaking with people. I would volunteer to go up to present my work in front of my class, read a passage from a text, or even ask a question. I think having this confidence helped me do better academically and socially. I begin to make new friends. They make class feel fun and not boring. I don't have to look at the clock every five minutes waiting for class to end. On weekends I would try and get out of the house any chance I got. I stopped playing video games as it reminded me of the times when I was unproductive and anti-social. I realized that I wanted to change the way I used my free time. My basketball coach once said, "The only way to get better at basketball is to play basketball." In order for me to get more comfortable with speaking with other people, I'd have to find people to talk to and have a conversation with them. So I started talking to more people at school, becoming good friends with them. They began to include me in their plans. I finally had friends that I could hang out with, that actually wanted to hang out with me. They'd text me, asking me if I'd like to go with them to get something to eat or go watch a movie. The moment I'd receive their text, my mood would go from a rain cloud to a bright sun. I'd instantly feel excited because I never got many chances to hang out with my friends outside of school. This feeling made me feel like I was starting to belong in a group. I finally felt like I fit in.

———

*Sally L. was born in San Francisco and is fifteen years old. She is an only child. She loves to play basketball. In the future, she hopes to start her own successful business. She likes to draw in her free time. Her favorite thing to do is spending time connecting with friends.*

# NEVER CHANGING

—

**WINSTON L.**

The storm in his heart blurs his mind,
always in the way,
always preventing him from thinking clearly,
always something on his mind.
He does not feel.

He walks a mile, one more left.

In his heart he sits in a room,
he walks out of the room into the storm,
he searches for self-love,
raindrops that fall hurt him like needles digging into his skin,
drenched in water, he turns back time.
Raindrops go up into a seamless, endless sky.
He looks upon himself yet again he is still wet.

He walks two miles, one more left.
He walks five, one more left.

Heart never changing, always the same
in the puddles he sees nothing
but past his lies and fake self
he finally sees who he is.

He stands there, one more mile.

———————

**Winston L.** *was born in San Francisco and is fifteen years old. He loves to be better. His favorite food is noodles. He has no plans. He dreams to not do any normal, boring job.*

# FRENEMIES

—

## RICKY L.

Gust dribbles the ball as the clock starts ticking down from ten. Gust starts getting nervous as the crowd starts counting down with the clock. While sweat is slowly dripping down his face and back, he hears the boos from the crowd. He mutters to himself, *Don't mess this up, Gust. Ignore the crowd.* He sees his best friend Rob wide open right in the paint and ready to make a layup, but Gust gets too nervous and just shoots the ball from the free throw line. Number twenty-three from the other team jumps up and misses the block. The crowd gets out of their seats from the moment the ball hits the rim and circles around. The ball doesn't go in and the buzzer goes off. They lost.

Everyone jumps up and cheers. Rob punches the wall while still on the court and goes into the locker room without shaking hands. Gust also runs into the locker room without shaking hands to see if he is okay. Rob sees Gust and yells, "Why didn't you pass me the ball? We could've won the game. I know you saw me, but I guess you were just trying to make a cool play. Well, tell you what…you didn't. And you lost us the game."

Gust tries to explain, but all that comes out his mouth is, "I-I-I w-w-as," and Rob just walks away angrily.

The next day at school, Rob says to Gust, "Sorry for what I did, and sorry for yelling at you. We cool now?"

Gust says, "It's aight," and they do their handshake and go to PE class together. Once they walk in, they see a new girl. Rob spots her right away and can't stop staring.

Rob says in an excited voice, "That's a beautiful girl."

Gust says, "Yeah, I guess," knowing in his head that if he said something else, Rob would get mad. The teacher blows his whistle and tells everyone to play basketball. Rob and Gust are happy because that is their favorite thing to do during the whole school day. Then they both see the girl playing basketball alone.

Rob says, "Psh, once she sees my basketball skills, she will fall right into my hands."

Gust replies with, "Bet: if you manage to get her to like you just because of your basketball skills, I'll buy you lunch."

Rob says, "Aight, say bye to your allowance then." Rob licks his fingers and fixes his eyebrows. He then runs his hand through his black hair before approaching her. He asks, "Do I look good right now?"

Gust giggles and says, "Sure." Rob approaches the girl all confident, walking one step at a time.

He then says to the girl, "Hey, pass me the ball. Let's play a game of horse and let's add a little spice to it. Whoever loses has to do something."

The girl shrugs and replies with, "Sure. My name is Nicki, by the way."

Rob says, "That's a nice name, but not as nice as my basketball skills." He then proceeds to shoot a three pointer and air balls.

Nicki giggles and says, "Aight, let's play. I'll go first." She then runs into the paint and does a simple layup.

Rob says, "Psh, you don't think I can do that?" He also does a layup. Nicki then grabs the ball and goes back into the paint, but this time it's different. She jumps up super high, puts the ball in between her legs, grabs it with her other hand, does a 360-degree turn and throws the ball up into the hoop. She makes it. Rob can't believe his eyes. He has never seen or done something like that before, but he does not want to lose the bet, so he says again, "Psh, I can easily do that," knowing that he can't.

He grabs the ball and approaches the paint. He jumps as high as he can and puts the ball in between his legs just like Nicki did, but he bends back too far and falls straight on his back.

Nicki approaches him and asks, "Are you okay?" Gust does the opposite and bursts out laughing.

Rob moans then gets up and replies to Nicki, "Ow, that hurt, but yeah, I'm good. I have to admit, you are really good at basketball. Did you play at your old school?"

Nicki then tells her story on how she got here. She says, "Yes, I actually used to be on the women's team at Buniton, a really good school with the best sports teams, but I got expelled. There was this one game that we had and there was a rumor going around that I would cheat by using shoes that gave me a lot more jump height. What I did not know was that the opposing team broke into my locker and replaced my shoes. I played in them and I didn't notice my jump height until I went for a layup and boom. I felt like an eagle with those shoes. They stopped the game instantly because it was so obvious, and then they checked my shoes. I was confirmed a cheater. The whole crowd went crazy and the other team got the victory instantly. My team got so pissed at me and I lost all of my friends right then and there. I got called into the office after the game knowing that I got set up and was done for. I sat down. The principal did not say anything and just handed me a paper. It was an expulsion form. I just sat there and tears started rolling down my face. They then proceeded to call my parents and even more tears started pouring out. I could hear my parents' whimpers on the phone call and I just ran out of the room and went straight home. My parents started yelling at me, talking about my future and everything. I swore to myself that I would never join another sports team again since it was what ruined my life."

Rob and Gust are really surprised and they never look at her the same way. Nicki changes the subject after that and says, "Can I be friends with you guys? I am new to this school and everything, so maybe you can help me?"

Gust says instantly, "Yes, I would love to be your friend." The bell rings after that and they all go to their classes.

After their classes, it's lunch time. Rob and Gust sit down in the cafeteria and bring out their lunches. Gust says, "Ha, you suck. I got pizza and you just got a stupid peanut butter sandwich."

Rob says, "Well, you're the one that is gonna get fat because that pizza is looking greasier than your face." They go on and on. Nicki spots them and sits right where they are. Rob sees her out of the corner of his eye and quickly kicks Gust on the leg. Rob says, "Oh, hey Nicki. You can sit with us."

She sits down laughing and says, "So how have you guys been?"

Gust says, "Gre—,"

Rob interrupts Gust, saying, "I have been great, Nicki. Has anyone ever told you that you've got nice eyes?"

Nicki replies with a confused face, "Um, not really. Thanks though, buddy."

Rob felt the pain once she said the word "buddy." His heart broke right there and he knew that he just got friend-zoned. He was having tons of thoughts rush him at that moment like, *Maybe she just said that because we just met* and *Was my compliment too much?*

Rob then finally gets some words out of his mouth after that and says, "Y-y-yeah, no problem," in a screechy voice. After that, they just talk and talk while lunch flies by. This group of friends had a connection. They were meant to be together. Lunch ends and they all go to class.

The school year passes and the group of friends gets closer and closer. One day, Gust has the flu. It is only Rob and Nicki together and they are having a conversation about food until Nicki randomly says, "You know, Gust is a really nice guy. I need some advice, Rob. I've liked Gust for a while now and I am planning to ask him out. Since you're his best friend, I was wondering if you have any tips for me." Once Rob hears this he just straight-up runs away, straight to the closest bathroom. Nicki is confused and thinks he just needed to use the bathroom really badly, so she just goes to class after that.

Rob is pissed after he hears that. He yells at himself. *How can she like Gust but not me?* He punches the walls and kicks the bathroom stalls.

The next day, Rob does not get out of his bed. He just stays there and wants to be there forever. He feels like he is done with life. Rob's mom tries to get him out of bed, but he won't budge until she goes to work. His grades are dropping and dropping. His basketball skills are also dropping and dropping.

At school it is only Gust and Nicki together, and they are really confused about where Rob went. They are getting really worried one day and decide to give Rob a visit at his house. Gust knocks on the door and then Rob screams, "Go away!"

Gust says, "Rob, what happened? Where have you been and why are you screaming at us?"

"Just please go away, I don't want to talk to either of you."

"What did we ever do to you?"

"You know what you did. Now listen to me: go away now!"

Gust says, "Hey, Nicki. Let's respect his property and leave," and they leave.

Nicki says while walking, "I really do wonder what happened to him. He's one of my best friends and I have never seen him this mad before."

"Neither have I, and I am definitely getting worried now."

"It's okay. Let's just hope he is doing fine."

The next day at school, Nicki decided to make her move for Gust. She has written a script in her head of how she was going to do it. It was during lunch when she sees Gust and approaches him slowly. They sat together at lunch like usual. But this time it was different. This time, Nicki sat beside Gust instead of across from him. Gust was confused, but he shrugged it off and proceeded to eat his lunch, a peanut butter sandwich. Nicki moves in closer, and Gust was even more confused.

Gust says, "Hey, Nicki. You are weirding me out. First you sit next to me instead of across from me, then you are now moving closer to me. What's going on?"

Nicki says, "Gust…I think I like you."

Gust says in a confused way, "Wait, what?"

"I just said I think I like you."

"Stop playing with me."

"I am serious, Gust, and I don't want to repeat myself." They both get as red as tomatoes now.

"Um, I mean, I don't really know what to say. Look, my best friend Rob likes you and I don't want to lose him as a friend, sorry."

Nicki gets really embarrassed and runs to the bathroom with her head down. Gust chases after her. Gust catches up to her and grabs her hand before she goes into the girls' bathroom.

Gust tells her, "Look, it's for the greater good. We both don't want to lose Rob as a friend. I really like you too, but we can't do anything about it."

Nicki, while still holding Gust's hand, goes in for a kiss and Gust accepts it.

Gust says, "Wow, I just can't help myself. I can't hold myself back, and I feel so guilty right now."

Nicki says, "It's okay. Don't let anyone stop you for who you like."

One day Rob eavesdrops on his mom, a biochemist, and hears her talk about a new flower she discovered. He hears that this flower, if mushed up and mixed with water, causes people to fall in love with the first person they see. An idea rings in Rob's head. He tells himself, *What if I give this to Nicki? I can finally get her!* He sneaks into his mom's room and looks everywhere. He then sees a suitcase and opens it. There is a pink, rose-looking flower. He grabs one of the petals, then closes the suitcase and leaves. Rob goes back to his room to make his creation. He mushes up the flower with his mug and puts its contents in a water bottle. He then fills up the water bottle and his operation is ready.

The next day, Rob goes to school ready to do his plan. When he arrives at school, he sees Gust and Nicki holding hands. This makes him even more mad and now he wants to execute his plan even more. Nicki and Gust spot Rob and they both say in a happy way, "HEY, ROB! YOU'RE BACK!" They were both so excited and hug Rob.

Gust says, "So, hey, what made you come back to school? Did you miss us too much?"

Rob says, "Psh, no I didn't miss anyone. I just got bored at home. Why would I miss you?"

Gust says, "Ha, I know you missed me, just admit it. But hey, welcome back to the group!"

Nicki says, "Hey, Rob. Long time no see. I see that you finally came back!"

Rob says, "You too, Nicki. I missed you. I made you some tea when I was home to apologize to you, Nicki." Rob hands Nicki the love potion.

Nicki says, "Aww, thank you, Rob. I actually forgot my water bottle today, so this sure will come in handy to quench my thirst." Nicki takes the tea and drinks it. She says right after, "Wow, this tea is good. It tastes like flowers! What did you put in it?" Nicki then makes eye contact with Rob and can't stop looking. Rob says nothing.

Gust says, "Hey, what is wrong, Nicki? You don't seem right. Why are you staring at Rob like that?"

## "I ruined my best friend's relationship and I can't believe that I would do such a thing."

Nicki then says, "I don't care if there is something wrong with me. All I care about is Rob!" Rob gets excited that the plan is working.

Rob says, "I know you care about me. Now come in here and give me a kiss." Nicki approaches Rob, but right when she leans in for a kiss, Gust pull her back.

Gust says, "What is wrong with you, Nicki? Are you joking around with him or what?"

Nicki replies with, "Why would I be joking? Rob is my true love and no one else is. No one can separate me from Rob."

Rob says, "Whoa, Nicki. You are going a bit crazy. You should turn it down a bit."

Nicki says, "What did you tell me to do? I will never turn down my love for you, Rob!" She then runs up to him and gives him a kiss. Gust doesn't say anything and runs up to his next class. He was done with Rob and Nicki.

Nicki then says, "Finally he is gone. Now we can love each other peacefully." Rob starts regretting everything he had said or done these past few days.

He says, "Hey, look Nicki, I messed up and gave you a love potion. I regret what I did and I know that both you and Gust like each other a lot. I don't want to change or affect anything in your relationship anymore. I am so sorry I did this. Just please go back to being regular."

Nicki ignores everything he said and says, "I love you, Rob. Just be with me. I don't care about anything else." Rob knows he messed up big time and he calls his mom to ask her how to cure the curse.

Rob's mom says, "There is no cure except for one way. Gust has to kiss her again."

Rob then runs up to Gust's classroom and drags Nicki with him. Rob drags Gust out to the hallway and talks to him. He says, "Gust, I gave Nicki a love potion and the only way to cure it is if you kiss her again. Look, I am sorry for what I did and I know that I messed up big time. Just please kiss her again. I ruined my best friend's relationship and I can't believe that I would do such a thing."

Gust says, "What? Are you playing around with me or something? You think I would believe that stupid fantasy that you made up?" He tries to go back into class but Rob grabs him.

Gust says, "Let go of me!"

Rob says, "I can't. Just please trust me here. I am sorry for everything I have done. Just kiss Nicki."

Gust sighs and says, "I love Nicki and you really had to take her away from me. What can I trust about you after what you've done? But I will trust you this time, because after all, you are my best friend."

---

*Ricky L. is from San Francisco and he has been here his whole life. He doesn't really have any hobbies because he just likes to do what's fun! He loves fun so much that it is his goal in life to have as much fun as possible. When he grows up and graduates, he wants to be a computer programmer.*

# CHANGE

—

## WILL L.

Goals. **Everyone has** them, big or small. In life, most people have dreams or goals they want to achieve one day. We make these goals when we are kids and throughout our adulthood.

To reach your goals, you must dedicate, adapt, and change yourself. Dedicating yourself means sacrificing unnecessary things that won't help you reach your goals. You also need to adapt in situations that don't go your way. This can teach you that nothing is given and that you can never expect everything to go your way. When you dedicate yourself and adapt to overpowering harsh obstacles, you'll eventually start to change and head down the right path to your goals.

Disciplined people may not think this process is hard, but it isn't as easy for everyone. Some people who have big goals can't change themselves, which makes their goals seem unreachable. Changing can be difficult because you might need to sacrifice things you like or do things you do not feel like doing. Often, your biggest obstacle to achieving your goal can be yourself. You may not realize when you are giving yourself stress, anxiety, or pressure that causes you to procrastinate and, in the end, can lead to laziness.

This reminds me of when I was eleven years old and first saw Division I high school basketball players in a game. I was amazed at their talent. They were incredibly athletic and insanely accurate at shooting the ball.

Just seeing such talented players going up against each other became an exciting game to watch. From that day, I wanted to be like them, or even better. I started playing basketball every day, and by middle school, others would say, "Whoa, he's pretty good." Everyone began having high expectations of me. I started to think that I was so good that I didn't need to practice as much, that no one was as good as I was and that becoming a Division I player would be easy.

That was when I started to become lazy. In my head, I thought, *Man, this sport is becoming too easy. No one can be better than I am. I should take some days off and just relax instead of playing every day.* Over the years, some of my classmates became as talented as I was. They rarely missed their shots. *Since when was he that good?* I asked myself. This surprised me and motivated me to become even better. But there was a problem: whenever I told myself to practice, I wouldn't do it. I would tell myself I'll do it another day.

The problem got worse. The same thing happened to my grades as well. I started becoming lazier and procrastinating. I realized I wasn't improving as much as I wanted to on my basketball skills, and my grades started to become worse and worse. I began feeling stress and anxiety because I was afraid that I wouldn't be as good as I wanted to be and that people were putting extreme pressure on me since they expected more from me.

At this point, I was done with middle school and realized what had to be done. I needed to change, because if I remained the same I wouldn't go anywhere. Throughout summer I wanted to change, but it wasn't easy because laziness stuck with me. I only worked out on the days that I felt motivated, either by a video or with my friends.

However, after summer, things didn't become easier. I had a grade point average of 2.0, and I wasn't as good in basketball. Eventually, I felt so much pressure and stress that I started practicing a lot, but I didn't see myself getting much better. I also tried to change my grades, but didn't get far. I had become noticeably better, but it was still far from where I wanted to reach. Going into sophomore year, I had been confident that I would do well in school, and that I would do so well in basketball games that everyone would know my name. *This is my year,* I told myself, *This is just another small milestone to becoming great. This is my year to become a top high school player.* In truth, I was really in over my head because I have remained the same: my grades are still bad, and I generally still don't do as well in basketball. In the end, I still haven't changed.

Now, I'm in the middle of sophomore year, and basketball season is almost over. But I'm still trying to change. I have friends who will point out my weaknesses and push me when I become lazy. So far, I see myself making some progress. I see myself adapting more to working hard and realizing everything is part of the process of becoming better. I want to change, but I don't have to do it all on my own. I am grateful to have friends who are willing to help. That is why I don't want to let them down, and plan to work harder and harder until I finally reach my goals.

---

*Will L.* was born San Francisco and is fifteen years old. He lives with a mom and an uncle. He loves to hang out with friends, play basketball, explore places, and sleep. His goal has to do with basketball in the future. He plans to get noticed by colleges.

# GOOD FRIENDSHIP VS. BAD FRIENDSHIP

—

## LAURA TUN M.

Dear Mom,

I'm writing you this letter because I want to let you know how thankful I am because you helped me through this situation. I remember the time I was talking to you about my middle school friends that I met, and I told you about this one girl the most because she was leading me through bad situations and involving me in them. To be honest, Mom, I'm not the type of girl that likes to have a lot of friends because you've taught me, given me examples, and told me that friends are bad and they will always get me in trouble. But on the other hand, you've told me, "Not all friends are the same and not all have bad intentions." The other thing you've taught me is to not make them friends and just make them classmates from school. Thanks to all that, Mom, when I was in middle school, I decided to put up a wall and stop talking to her because I wasn't going to tolerate a friendship like that. If I ever trip for another experience like that one, I'll be prepared. It won't be hard to cut a friendship even though it was hard to cut this one.

I remember that one time when we were both sitting down during class and she asked me who I had a crush on, so I told her because I trusted her. After days passed by, she told me she had a crush on the same boy I liked. I got so mad and I stopped talking to her. That same day she texted me asking if we could have a talk. And I told her, "No!" She texted begging, so I did accept to talk to her at last. After all the talk we had and all the times she said "sorry" and I accepted, she just kept doing the same thing over and over again. When she would ask me stuff after that, I just wouldn't tell her. I felt so mad because I thought I could trust her. This betrayal caused a boundary to be put up because she already had me irritated, and also because now I just wanted to shut her out.

Mom, I'm going to tell you the short story of the day when she told me to ditch class with her. One day, we were about to go to second period and we had class together. My phone was on silent and I felt it vibrate because it was in the left pocket of my jacket. She texted me saying, "I don't feel like going to class for second period."

I texted her saying, "Mannn…same here, but we have to go."

Then she texted again saying, "Ditch with me."

I said, "Nahhh, I'm good."

After that, she asked "Why?" and I just left her on delivered.

When I was walking to class, I didn't expect to see her because I never usually do, but I did. Anyway, she dragged me to the bathroom with her. After that, I walked out of the bathroom so someone could at least tell me to go to class. A teacher told me to, so I told her, "Eyy, I'll meet you in class."

And since she knew it was a teacher that told me, she said, "Okay." After this happened, I didn't want to see her during passing periods anymore because I didn't want her to drag me to the bathroom again. If no teacher came, I would've just let her stay mad and left her alone because for me at that time I just didn't want to get in trouble. I ignored her because I just didn't want to be led down bad paths.

Mom, I have to thank you because since that day she called your phone and thought I picked up, and she started saying things she would do that are dangerous, you told her that if she kept telling me about all those things you'd let the police know. Mom, I didn't want to put our family at risk for so many reasons. I felt that I had no fear, but at the same time, I did worry because I remember you told me that the writing prints of the letter were left on the notebook she wrote it on. I still remember how you reacted to the call. Mom, you got so mad and worried because you just didn't want me to go through a hard situation. We both talked about it and everything went well. I told you everything I had to tell you and you gave me advice on everything. You told me to stop talking to her slowly so that at first, she would not notice, and there would be no problems.

Mom, not talking to her was easy for me because you and I talked about it, and also because I was already so annoyed of everything she did. First, I tried to like for real, for real fix and restart this friendship by talking with my ex-best friend about this situation, and it seemed like she cared about restarting the friendship, but at the same time, it seemed like she didn't. The second thing I did was stop hanging out with her at school and over the weekend. The third thing I did was start to be less close to her. So, for example, when she would ask me about my personal life, or me and my boyfriend, I would just start to laugh and change the topic or just ignore her and tell her that I would let her know later. The fourth thing I did was block her from social media and also block her number. Mom, when she would ask me why I blocked her, I would just tell her that I decided to delete my accounts. To be honest, it seemed suspicious, but I really wanted the best for me and our family. I especially wanted to have the rest of my middle school with no drama. The fifth thing I did was stop smiling at her when she would smile at me so now we don't talk anymore. Mom, all of this ended! So, for seventh and eighth grade, my school year ended with no drama. Honestly, I never wanted to lose her as a best friend because it seemed like she was a real one. At the beginning we were like sisters.

Mom, from this experience I've learned that having bad friends only leads you to many problems, and they completely change your life. I've also learned to not keep secrets from you, Mom, so when I need you, you'll be there for me. I think that people do relate to this situation because I remember that one day I was listening to your conversation with our neighbor, and she was telling you the story about her daughter and how her best friend led her to bad things and that now she regrets everything and the trust she gave her. This border is important to me because it will be useful in the future. Mom, I was able to get over this border and what's next is to not trust anyone, and to not make the girls from school friends, and to only make them classmates for school and nothing else.

Mom, I'm writing you this letter because you taught me that bad friends can lead to bad paths, and to not follow any of them. Now I feel that when I have my own kids, I will tell them the exact same advice you gave me because it truly helped me. And it's still helping me through high school because now I know who to start to talk to and who not to. By that I mean I know at first connection. When a new person first starts talking to you, you can tell by the way they talk, the way they act, and what they talk about, whether or not they would be a good friend. If they talk about school stuff, they're good friends. If they talk about bad stuff, they're bad friends. For example, if they use bad words a lot when they express themselves, they are bad friends. If they are good friends, they would be helpful and the way they express themselves would be different. Life has taught me so many things, and in bad situations you've always been there for me, so I just wanted to say thanks and much love, Mommy.

Sincerely,
Your daughter

———

*Laura Tun M.* *was born in Mexico and is sixteen years old. She likes to listen to music and hang out with her friends and boyfriend. She wants to go to college and make her parents proud. She listens to trap music in Spanish. She has a big sister, a baby sister, and a brother.*

# ILLUDERE

—

## JAEDYN N.

"They say I'm living in my own reality. Throwing everything that bites me, even money. I wanna sit back, and set myself free. Set myself free, set myself free." —Veorra, Set Free

As I studied the movements of my hand in the air, I couldn't help but feel stuck. I'd been lying in bed for hours and hours, going back and forth between staring at my hands and staring at the cold concrete walls of this room, studying their tiny cracks and patterns, hoping that if I stared at them long enough I would somehow find the answers to my questions about this place.

*How can something be so perfect yet so flawed?*

I guess that's the funny thing about this city. Like DNA, the perfect world isn't necessarily perfect. If anything, it's riddled with flaws. Some people choose to ignore its defects, while others only see its imperfections. The more you try to make it seem perfect, the more problems you encounter. One of the many reasons why utopias don't exist.

"Understand I'm talking to the walls." —Harry Styles, Ever Since New York

**August 6, 2018, 10:30 a.m.**

"Welcome to Los Angeles," I heard a voice say. At first, I thought it was my mom saying something, so I took off my headphones and looked over at her to make sure that she wasn't talking to me, but she wasn't. It was just the GPS. So I put my headphones back on and resumed my music.

**"Where we're from, there's no sun, our hometown's in the dark. Where we're from, we're no one, our hometown's in the dark." —Twenty One Pilots, Hometown**

There was a knock on the door. "Come in, it's unlocked," I said while peering out the window, staring at the still city.

"You wanted to talk?" I heard a voice say. I turned around to face my guest.

"Hey, X. I've been wondering...have you ever been outside the city walls, or ever wanted to leave?"

"Whoa, no way. Of course not. You know that leaving is against the rules. Besides, I like it here. It feels comfortable. Safe." X explained. "Where is this even coming from?"

"I mean, come on. Don't you want to know what's out there?" I asked.

"Not really, no. I'm sure whatever's out there isn't gonna be much better than what's in here. Not only that, you know what happens to people who have attempted to leave? They all failed."

"But what about *them?*"

"For all you know, *they* don't even exist. Maybe they're just some fictional characters who were put into our books. I don't know, they seem like bad people. Ungrateful, really. I mean, they were given everything that one could possibly wish for: a roof over their heads, basic necessities, safety within these walls, and they choose to throw it all away. And for what? A chance to see the outside? The same things going on in here? Look, once you set foot out there, you'd want to come back here. You'll be hunted. They'll want to bring you back to the city, and chances are, they won't be bringing you back to this room."

"Don't you see what's wrong about everything you just said? They're taking away our freedom! So, what if I do make it out there? I can be free from this tiny prison of a room. At least if I were to get caught and brought back, I would finally get a change in surroundings."

"Listen, I'm not oblivious to all the messed up things about this place. What I'm trying to do is keep you safe, and the best way to do that is to keep you here. There's nothing out there for you. It's dangerous. You don't know anything about it other than what you've seen in books. You'll be better off here instead of out there."

We sat there in silence. I didn't know how to respond. A part of me agreed with what X had just said, but another part of me was curious. I wanted to know what it was like out there—if it was dark and gloomy like it is here, or if it was bright and sunny. I wanted to know what the weather was like—if it was cold, cloudy, and foggy like it is here, or if it was different. Maybe the sun is out there somewhere. Maybe it was warm and welcoming, just like how it is described in the stories told to us when we were young.

"I should leave. I have something to do," X said after a long moment.

"Oh, yeah. Sure. Thanks for coming," I replied, absentmindedly, while lost in my thoughts.

**"In my mind, I thought that the birds would sing and sparks would fly, but it's just quiet. Am I cruel? Or am I ignorant? Or was I fooled by the stories I knew?" —AJR, Turning Out**

**August 6, 2018, 12:47 p.m.**

"So, what do you think you'd want to do in the future?" my mom asked, interrupting my daydream.

"Um, probably something in film, like directing, writing, or video effects editing."

"What do you mean?" my mom asked me.

Because of my lack of Vietnamese vocabulary, I wasn't sure how to explain those things to her, so I decided to look up pictures on Google images to show her later on. As I scrolled and scrolled through the different search results, I found myself imagining the different things that I wanted to do in the future. I imagined myself making films, seeing my ideas come to life. The thought of it was definitely intriguing, though also scary, because I didn't know where to start. I had to do my own research and become more independent, since none of my family members went in the direction of filmmaking or anything close to that, so I haven't been able to ask any of them for help. I'm basically on my own.

**"You will hide from everyone, denying you need someone to exterminate your bones." —Twenty One Pilots, Friend Please**

After days of thinking and planning my escape, I decided that if I wanted to get out, I would have to do it by myself. So, I started to pack my things. I searched my belongings for items to bring along with me on my journey when I finally left.

I finished packing and started making my way down to the west entrance. I found out from my research that it's the one entrance that wasn't heavily guarded all the time. The air outside felt chilly. It was a cloudy day, no sign of the sun, like always. I walked past the tall gray buildings and the giant lifeless trees that never swayed because there was never a breeze. Everything was still as if it was stuck in place. It felt as though I was the only thing moving in this city.

After ten minutes of walking, I reached the gate, and like I suspected, there were no guards around, just a wall towering over me. I looked up and around to make sure that no one was watching me from their windows or following me, but all I found were closed, uninterested windows and vacant streets. I then focused my attention once again on the opening in the wall before me. It was like a giant black hole pulling me in, making my feet move on their own. My walk turned into a run. After I had passed the gate, I kept running. I wanted to get as far away from those walls as possible. I wanted to get away from the people there, away from the boring lifestyle. I wanted to get far away from the life that I lived, away from the room that I've spent most of my life in. I wanted to be free. As these thoughts ran through my head, I didn't realize that someone had grabbed my arm until I found myself being pushed to the ground.

"What do you think you're doing?" I heard a voice say, as I struggled to catch my breath. "You're not supposed to be here."

I looked up and saw a person wearing peculiar clothing that I had never seen before in my life. He was wearing a large black jacket, black pants, and old worn-down shoes. Under his jacket was a red hoodie which covered his head and a bandana shielding everything but his eyes. On his left arm was an armband with a logo consisting of three strangely shaped triangles intertwined within each other, and next to it the word "illudere" which meant to create an illusion. Then it hit me, he was one of *them*.

"Hey! Did you hear what I just said?" He asked, interrupting my thoughts.

"Let go of me!" I demanded, as I struggled out of his grasp. "I'm trying to leave."

"If you're trying to leave, then maybe you should look at where you're going." The stranger moved aside so that I could see the massive army of guards standing there in their white clothing. "You're walking straight into a trap."

"But I thought there were no guards around here. I did my research; they shouldn't be here at all," I tried to argue.

"That's where you're wrong. They keep guards here to trick kids like you. Escaping isn't that easy."

I stood there stunned. He was right. It was too easy.

"Look, if you want to leave, come with me. We can help you."

"Who are you?" I asked, suddenly realizing that I didn't even know his name.

"I'm Adrian and these are my friends," he said pointing to a small group of about ten people in the same peculiar clothing. "Follow me, I'll show you the safest way out."

I stared blankly at him. I didn't know how to respond. *Do I trust these people? Why are they trying to help me? How do I know they're not just guards in disguise?* Soon, I was drowning in these types of questions. I felt paralyzed, not being able to decide on whether or not I should trust them. Maybe I was overthinking it. Maybe they're nice people who are just trying to help out.

"Well?" Adrian asked, once again breaking the silence and disrupting my train of thought.

"Oh, um, yeah. Sure. After you." I nodded and followed them, still skeptical nonetheless.

**"Let's go out in flames so everyone knows who we are 'cause these city walls never knew that we'd make it this far. We've become echoes, but echoes that faded away." —Aquilo, Silhouettes**

August 6, 2018, 6:23 p.m.

After hours and hours of following the GPS, my family and I finally reached the hotel that we were staying at. We got out of the car and began bringing our luggage up to our room. As my parents unpacked their suitcases, I decided to sit on one of the beds to read my book and listen to some music. It didn't last long, though, because after a few minutes, I was already drifting off to sleep.

**"No, I don't know which way I'm going, but I can hear my way around." —Twenty One Pilots, The Hype**

"You're on your own now. Just step through there and you'll be outside." Adrian said, pointing at the light shining through the opening in the wall. I turned around to thank him, but he was gone. I then made my way toward the opening.

I closed my eyes for a moment, hesitant, but when I finally opened them again, I felt it—the sun on my face, its warmth. And for the first time in my life, I felt joy, inexplicable happiness. I smiled as I felt the weight of fears and doubts lifted off my shoulders. The clouds covering my vision were now gone. I saw the world for the first time. It was breathtaking.

Then, I was left with the question of *What now?* There they were again: the fears, the doubts, the uncertainty washing over me as I stared into the big open world ahead of me. My mind raced with so many questions. *Where do I go from here?* At this moment, I felt lost, unsure of what to do next. All my life I had things planned out for me. I had a routine. I did the same things every single day, but now, *now* I don't have to do anything, I don't have to follow anyone's orders. I am free, and though the thought of being able to do whatever I wanted was intriguing and exciting, it was also scary and didn't feel safe.

I felt torn between two worlds. In one world, I was safe and comfortable, but at the same time, I was stuck. And in the other, I was free and in control, yet I didn't feel like I was in control; I felt vulnerable and confused.

I was so lost in my thoughts that I didn't hear the sound of footsteps coming toward me. I froze, unsure of what to do, but as they became louder and louder, I followed my first instinct and I ran. I ran and ran until my feet hurt, until my lungs felt like they were about to catch on fire. I ran to the rhythm of my own heartbeat, pounding on and on as if it was trying to escape my chest. I ran so fast I couldn't even think, I had left my thoughts behind, all the fears, all the doubts, the only thing on my mind was how much I had run.

*Faster, faster, come on, faster,* I kept repeating to myself.

The burning sensation in my lungs as I tried to fill them with air had become too much to bear, and before I knew it, I was crying. Tears blurred my vision; I couldn't see where I was going, but it didn't stop me from moving forward. Even then, all I wanted to do was give in. I wanted to stop, to go back to that room, back to those walls. I wanted to give up. The next thing I knew, my feet had tangled together and I tripped. But before I was able to make contact with the ground, someone had caught me.

"Come on, you're almost there." I heard one voice say. "You've made it this far, don't fall back now."

"Keep going," said another.

Not long after, there was a chorus of voices encouraging me to keep moving. Soon these words began giving me hope. I was going to make it.

**"Lyrics that mean nothing. We were gifted with thought. Is it time to move our feet to an introspective beat? It ain't the speakers that bump hearts. It's our hearts that make the beat." —Twenty One Pilots, Holding On To You**

---

*Jaedyn N. was born in Ho Chi Mihn City, Vietnam. She is fifteen years old. She lives with her mom and dad. She likes to draw, read, and listen to music. She wants to work in the film industry in the future.*

# INCOMPLETE

—

## NATHAYA O.

"Ho lang."

I was confused because I didn't understand what was said and I knew he was talking about me because whenever he spoke in Cantonese, he would say something so I couldn't understand. So, then I ignored him and continued doing my geometry homework.

He interrupted me and said, "Why are you always mad?"

I responded calmly, "I'm not...just doing my homework." He continued talking back to me. I couldn't deal with him anymore. I felt my body heating up and the ends of my fingertips gripping on my pencil. He was so annoying. He always had something to say, like I was a threat to him, and he made me lose focus on my homework, and so then I stood up from my chair and left. As I left Sweetheart Cafe and walked through Chinatown, I could feel the rain running down my face as I looked up at the blank, dark sky. I felt so unconnected to my friends, the people around me.

I finally arrived at my warm happy shell. Right when I stepped into it, I could smell cinnamon. I knew exactly what my mom was making: *Kai Pa Lo.* It's a dish to eat over rice. When you open the lid of the pot, you smell cinnamon mixed with palm sugar and see eggs, tofu, beef, and all sorts of spices. The strongest smell was the cinnamon. I rushed into the kitchen and spoke in Thai, asking if dinner was ready. I felt safe in this place I call home. I felt accepted here, and no one could judge me from how different I am because we all speak Thai. Although I still remembered the feeling of heat running through my body, I couldn't let what happened today bother me because I noticed how unique I am. I could speak an amazing language that barely any of my friends spoke, and I came home to a spectacular meal. I thought to myself, *I am a Thai, Chinese American girl, who has no clue how to speak Chinese, but at the same time I'm proud to be at home where there are people I can connect with personally and emotionally.*

When I got into my room, I saw a poster I made in kindergarten and it reminded me of the time at school we'd talked about all sorts of things, like where my family came from, my family background, and family tree, but I'd always get stuck. That made me start wondering about who I am. I knew I was so different from everyone else. My parents both came from different regions of Thailand. There's not a lot to say about my Chinese side of the family because my parents rarely talked about it, but I knew that my great grandfather sailed a boat from China and helped build the foundation of the city hall near my mom's hometown. I have this whole side of the family and yet I never heard anyone speak Chinese, though my mom and her siblings use Chinese terms to refer to each other. Other than that, we all speak English and Thai.

On a sunny day, my family and I decided to go to Water World to spend quality time with each other. My cousins and I talked about all sorts of things, like what we liked—for example, One Direction, because at the time my cousin Amy liked them. All of us were talking. I talked to my other cousins in Thai, but Amy didn't speak Thai fluently. She told me, "Never stop speaking Thai, because you will regret it in the future." She wished she spoke more Thai because she would be able to communicate with our family. She told me to be proud of who I'd become because if I stopped speaking Thai, it would be like losing a part of myself, my identity.

I've been setting goals lately. I set a goal last month to drink more water, and I wrote a reflection about my experience and I told myself that if I set my mind to do it, I could push myself. I can set a long-term goal on learning how to speak Mandarin or Cantonese. I don't think learning a language will help me know more about my family, but it will make me fit in more with my friends. I am going to continue speaking Thai and English, because those are my first and second languages and they are part of my identity. I haven't achieved the goal of learning Mandarin or Cantonese yet, so my story is incomplete.

———————

**Nathaya O.** *was born in San Francisco and is sixteen years old. She is Thai and Chinese. She loves to play football. Her favorite colors are blue, yellow, and red. One day, she hopes to become a pilot and travel the world. She has two half-brothers, and one is part German, Thai, and Chinese. Her parents came from different parts of Thailand. She loves chicken.*

# LA VIDA DE UNA MUJER

—

## MAYBELLIN R.

Men feed off of believing they are better than women. I was taught this at a very young age, that I was not allowed to even speak up to men when they hurt me. Our whole lives as women we are forced to accept we can never reach the same power as men. The phrase, "You are not as strong as men," can overpower us and those men love when women give up. As women, we are not allowed to love ourselves, to explore our minds, but doing so will give us the strength to make that inequality disappear. Mama taught me to never let a man put you down. She taught me independence. When life is throwing hardships at you, Mama taught me, through her example, to stand up tall and push through.

I first became aware of this border between men and women when I was seven years old. It was one crazy night. Mama had been working at Costa Del Sol from 8:00 a.m. to 12:00 a.m., and I was there sitting by the register area, waiting for her to tell me, *"Amor, tu papa esta aqui."* The odor of *pupusas* and seafood floated toward hungry customers, filling the restaurant. My eyes felt like weights—I kept falling asleep every thirty seconds. I saw her twirl all around the restaurant, but she never twirled toward me. Finally, I got the courage to go ask her what time Papa was coming. She said, *"No se, mija.* Go tell your brother to call him." Sitting next to me at the register, my brother called Papa, then looked at me with those big, light brown eyes and told me that Papa didn't answer. I sat back down and took a nap with all the noise of the dishes banging everywhere, everyone talking to each other as if they were deaf, and all I could think of was why he hadn't answered us.

# "Mama taught me to never let a man put you down."

I woke up from my mama shaking me, saying Papa was here. I was so excited yet so tired, so I grabbed my backpack and went outside the restaurant, into his car. I was too tired to even say hi to Papa. I saw the time was 2:00 a.m. I saw Mama coming toward us, swaggering with anger. I felt her energy, a woman who worked day and night and had had enough of a man who was drinking day and night. In a low voice, Mama asked him why he was late again, then, slowly getting louder, why he smelled like alcohol knowing he had to pick up his kids. Papa tried to tell her he had been working really late, that he lost track of time, but Mama could smell the lies coming out of him. They both have this fire inside of them. Papa was in a rage because Mama wasn't falling for his lies. He was so adjusted to women falling for his web of lies, but she's smarter than he is. That's when Papa hurt Mama. I was so afraid, I couldn't move. My brother ran inside the restaurant and waved his hands to get my family to help. I saw all the power Papa had with his hands as well as with his words. I didn't want to view Papa as an angry, aggressive, and manipulative man, but he made that border.

Men are misusing their power. We're taught that men are always right, always smart, always successful in life. My story shows you that not all men are that ideal stereotype. This is not a hate letter for men. This is just about awareness to treat each other as valuable human beings without a border between. My mom didn't give up that night, she used all that pain to lift herself up. She ended up going to nursing school to support our family. My mom proved to me that although I am a woman and men will view us as weak and sensitive, she told me to always stand up for myself. Mama is a powerful woman who already crossed that border, and I am next in line.

------------

*Maybellin R.* *was born in San Francisco. She is sixteen years old. She loves reading poetry and listening to music. One day, she hopes she can help people around the world. She is currently doing an internship with UCSF, a program where you talk about the struggles women face. Pizza and pasta are her favorite foods.*

# FAMILY TREE

—

## VINCENT W.

It was 7:00 p.m., but the sky was completely dark outside. You could only see the rain by the yellow light of the streetlamp outside of Johnny's apartment. Usually we played video games, but that night we worked on a lab report due the next Monday. As we worked, I thought of how my mom would be mad at me because she thought that we were playing, when in reality we were worn down by the formulas on the screen of Johnny's computer.

"My mom called me again and she told that I have to go soon. I mean, it's also pouring and dark outside. Besides, I'm done with my homework, so I'll go home and we'll play then."

"Do you really have to go? Why does your mom have to be so strict?" Johnny said, clearly annoyed that we didn't get as much time as we had wanted.

I never really knew how to explain to my mom what I did by translating from English to Chinese, so she always assumed that it was all lies to play games. She would warn me with punishments such as locking the door to the apartment in the building and keeping it that way with the silent treatment. It wasn't just playing games she was worried about, but also the fact that it was dark out and if unlucky, the pouring rain that happened once in a while would catch me. I had explained to her that today was a Friday, which meant that tonight was not a school night.

By the time Johnny and I were finally satisfied with the result of our typed lab report, it was already past 8:00 p.m. The discussion of what we would do that night and the following day ended in minutes as to save time while I carefully put on my rain shoes and backpack, knowing that the rain would hit hard the whole time I walked home. Johnny and I said our goodbyes and with a swift motion I opened my umbrella and propped it on my shoulder right as I stepped out. My mom's warnings again filled my mind, causing me to frown slightly and quicken my pace into the darkness of night.

The rain continued blanketing the streets as I turned the corner from the two-way alleyway Johnny's apartment was located on. I was well aware that my mom would call me while I was on my way back, the only time that I don't check my phone, but I also knew that this scenario has happened enough for my mom to know why I didn't answer. Once in a while I would look down at my waterproof shoes, satisfied that my socks stayed completely dry—unlike the previous night, when I was limping from the endless amount of water that had seeped through my running shoes quickly and easily, as if my shoes were only paper towels wrapped around my feet. After walking fast for a while in the dull roaring of the rain and wind, I managed to make it back to my apartment building. I had forgotten to put my keys in my pocket like almost every other time, as if my reminder to do so was on a whiteboard and someone had erased it in one quick swipe, which meant I had to strain to turn my backpack around with an umbrella. The lock to the outside door unlocked from my key and I quickly went in, closing the umbrella as swiftly as I had opened it to leave. Climbing the steps to my apartment on the top floor was more of a workout than usual, but I was just grateful to be under the protection of a roof. I got to my door, and reached out with my key, hoping I would not have to beg to get in.

\* \* \*

I've been aware of this ever since I was a kid, struggling to balance English with both Cantonese and Mandarin while doing almost everything my mom told me to do. At first it was fun and games, joking around about how I didn't know some words in the opposite language, and just doing what my mom told me without much thought. But as I moved on to middle school, many things I did became independent, such as going to and leaving school. This transition was the seed from which my mom's concern sprouted, but she did not think much about it because I followed my older sister to school and went to an afterschool program right when the bell rang. Only a year later, my sister graduated to high school, and again my mom's concern grew.

A year ago, I had stopped using my hall locker. I did this because I saw it as more convenient, carrying all my books to my classes so I never had to go to my locker for certain things. It was also a good workout for my shoulders, and was considered a part of my daily exercise. When this became clear to my mom, she felt the opposite of how I felt.

"Why are you carrying both textbooks back home? Why are you so dumb?" she would say every time I returned home from school.

"I am not dumb to do this. It is convenient. What if I have textbook work for more than one class and I only have one textbook?" I retorted.

In the end I agreed to leave some things at home. No matter how minor of an issue something is, take for example the textbooks, it splits my mom and me apart even if it is for a temporary amount of time. Even though this concern for me caused conflicts such as these, I knew deep down that she did things for my own good, for my well-being, no matter how rough it was on the outside. I knew of this love-hate connection, but to this day I am still trying to fully understand the love part on the inside while at the same time tolerating the hate side which showed often among our family.

Conflicts sometimes don't even happen on purpose, but from misunderstandings and the different languages in general. If and when I translate something wrong or not translate enough, my mom would take it seriously and again tension would fill the area between us. I would be angry at her for not understanding how my life goes academically and socially. She would be upset at me for similar reasons, but against the other culture/language. This misunderstanding figuratively and literally is also a big contributor to her concern.

This has been going on for my whole life. Even now there are still small slivers of tension in our conversations, as if the roots of nearby trees tangled with each other in an effort to get more area. It has been sixteen years since my life began, and yet I have never gotten to experience the world. I never rode on a plane or train. I never traveled farther than California or stayed out of S.F. for more than a few days. She has suppressed my freedom the moment I got it in middle school. But I have learned to live with it and to be honest. It makes me who I am now. I may accept the way things are going, but without my mom's restrictions, I could be out in the world, learning more, doing more. As much as I am being held back, I am who I am and this is the life I accept and will live.

The key entered the keyhole and turned, then pushed forward. The door creaked open to reveal the hallway that connected all of the apartment's rooms. I went to the living room to drop off my backpack, then to the bathroom to drop off my umbrella. Finally, I went to the kitchen and up to my mom.

"I'm back from doing homework. Sorry for taking so long," I said, hoping to not be ignored.

She nodded with approval, and I turned around to go change.

*It's nice to know our connection will stay the same to keep our family together; and like much of my current life, it's rarely changing, just the way I like it,* I thought, relieved that her tree of concern was slowly tilting over and dying.

---

**Vincent W.** *was born in San Francisco with parents that immigrated to America. Due to the presence of discipline, he took up a hobby for reading in middle school. With some help, he was able to write and publish his first book in high school.*

# DECISIONS

—

## RYAN Y.

Homeroom: a place where students go in between classes to take a break. Like all days when I had homeroom, it was a noisy place where students would sit down and chat with their friends, do homework, or just play on their phones. Each homeroom was unique, with different teachers that taught different subjects. My homeroom was a chemistry lab with beakers, test tubes, valves, and chemical equipment scattered all over the place. Every week we had a broadcast on this old TV where students in the Media Arts pathway would create shows that reflected upon previous events or just creative ideas that they thought of. I was talking to my friends when my homeroom teacher started to pass out sheets of paper. I realized that it was March, the time when students were given classes to choose for the following year. Grabbing one of the many sheets that were passed out, a wave of anxiety and a jolt of fear rushed down my spine like a waterfall as I confirmed my own thoughts. I looked over to my friends who also picked up the sheets. Unlike what I had felt, they continued to tell jokes and laugh while I was there contemplating what to do. At that point, the bell rang, breaking me out of the sudden trance. I quickly stuffed the form into my folder for later as I started to walk to my next class.

The next time I pulled out the form was at home, on my desk with a lamp illuminating the smooth, black, wooden surface. I'd recently finished my homework and had nothing planned. For me, home was a place where I could relax and concentrate on the things I needed to do like homework, chores, and if I had the time, probably reading or video games. Pulling out my form, I slowly looked at the options. There were many categories that separated the types of classes that I could take, such as English, History, Visual & Performing Arts, etc. While I was given the freedom to choose my classes, I was required to take certain ones in order pass high school. However, I did have the option to choose harder versions known as "Honors" or "Advanced Placement" (AP) classes. One by one, I looked through each class that was available to me, checking off the ones that I wanted to take. I decided to go with English I, Algebra II, Geometry I, AP World History, Chemistry, and Chinese. While I was choosing, I was also thinking about the consequences. For instance, Chemistry was one of the more problematic choices. I wanted to take Honors Chemistry, but I began to think that it was going to be a lot of work, and along with AP World History, that would be too much for me to handle. *Should I do this? Is this going to be too much?* Those types of thoughts were flowing through my head, causing me to feel that fear and anxiety from earlier, along with a new feeling: confusion. Exhausted and conflicted, I put the sheet back into my folder for another time.

As a child from an Asian family, I was told to excel at whatever I was doing. Whether it was chores, homework, or everyday things, it had to be good. During this process of choosing classes, I was told by my friends, parents, and teachers to take AP or Honors classes so that I could create a better future for myself. I was in no position to ignore their suggestions given that they'd had experiences that I hadn't yet. They were important to me, helping me with work or giving little tidbits of advice that could be useful later on. My head was at a standstill, conflicted between the advice given by my peers and my own thoughts. I grew up thinking that any mistake meant failure, and from that, I began to develop a mindset that forced me to apply pressure onto myself at all times. This is how I developed the mental border that prevented me from making decisions.

I always think about the consequences before doing something, but fearing failure, I focus more on the negative side of things. I guess that's when this sort of doubt came about, this lack of self-confidence that has affected my decision-making.

Decisions are not easy. One wrong choice and your life could end up falling apart to the point where you just can't do anything. It could lead to more problems and more conflicts like how a chain is linked, leading to nothing but an endless pit. No way out until you are completely consumed by the darkness that is fear. For me, it was the decisions that really prevented me from moving forward.

A few weeks later, I pulled out the form once again. However, this time would be the last, as the deadline was approaching and classes had to be finalized. I sat at the wooden desk like before, but this time my personal laptop was in front of me. In my school, we had to submit our applications online before they were processed and our final schedules determined. I began to review what I had chosen. *Chemistry, the one class that was the most conflicting of all the choices. What if I don't like it? What if it's too easy? I'll take the risk and leave it as it is. The burden of taking Honors Chemistry and AP World History may be too much. Geometry and Algebra II are classes I want to take, so no problem there. AP World History: challenging, perhaps intriguing, and college credits will help save me money, so I'll take it. And Chinese is the language I speak at home, so better to take it than not. If I improve my Chinese, I may be able to form better connections with my parents. English is required, so no objections there. That's all I have. Am I sure of this? Don't be afraid, just do it.* Finishing up my thoughts, I began to input the selection of classes into the computer. Pressing submit, I felt relief as if I had figured out a math problem that was once too complex for me to understand. The classes weren't too easy to the point where I wouldn't be challenged, but they were also hard enough to cause me to think and to work with my maximum potential. From that day on, my school year went by in a breeze, and soon summer had arrived.

Summer is a time where students of all ages can pursue their interests or relax. You get this sort of freedom that pushes away the fears and the worries of the school year into the back of your head. We have this large period of time where we can just enjoy ourselves. Before I knew it, summer was coming to an end and I had to go to school once again. Our schedules were mailed to us earlier, containing the six classes that I had chosen the previous semester. Anxiety and fear quickly replaced my calmness, causing my head to be all over the place. *Is this really going to be fine? Will this be enjoyable? What if I don't like my classes? Are there any alternatives if not? Is it even possible to transfer?* However, I thought back to when I had submitted my classes and that feeling of relief that came afterwards. Pushing away the fear, I started to walk to my first class of the day.

The day went by quickly, with teachers introducing themselves and passing out multiple syllabi. My earlier anxiety and fears began to dissipate as I went from class to class. I liked some of the classes, for instance AP World History, which I thought would be a lot of work and challenging. It was challenging and had a heavy workload, but it also seemed fun. Classes weren't normally fun, as they could be more serious and focus on helping you improve, but sometimes teachers had this sort of teaching style which caused students to enjoy themselves. In my AP World class, we discussed and talked about each chapter that we read, however in some cases we had quizzes or games that helped us remember important details. These quizzes or games challenged and helped us learn in a more engaging and fun way, as we discovered more and tested ourselves at the same time. However, there were also classes that I didn't really like during my first week. Chemistry, one of the choices I had had trouble with, was simply too easy for me. I wanted to take Honors Chemistry, but like before, I thought it contained too much work. For days, I spent time pondering this decision. More anxiety and a sort of pressure built up inside me, causing my head to hurt every time I thought about it. Remembering the advice given to me earlier, I finally decided to do it. Something inside me, whether it was myself or my instinct, told me, *You can do it. Just because there is a lot of work doesn't mean you'll fail. Just work harder and you'll eventually adapt and ascend past your current self.* Going to a previous teacher for help, he recommended that I talk to my homeroom teacher, as that was a more direct way to switch. I am very grateful for his help and all his encouragement, even to this day. So instead of requesting for a transfer, I went to my homeroom teacher who taught Honors Chemistry. I told him that I wanted to take his class as my current one wasn't hard enough. He was really helpful and told my counselor who swapped me into one of his Honors Chemistry classes. My previous teachers and my friends told me that he was going to be really difficult and that there was going to be a lot of work. I took their words and instead of putting myself down, I pushed forward. There was no going back now.

From then on, I began to work and work every day. Sometimes my hands feel like they're on fire from all the writing, but I still do it. Sometimes I have so much homework that it affects my sleep, but I still finish it. Through all this hard work, I have made many mistakes and errors. Back then, I would get mad at myself for missing even a single problem, but now that I have accumulated a huge amount of work, I've begun to accept the mistakes and errors. A new mindset has developed from it, one that makes me accept the fact that no one is perfect and that I can instead use the mistakes to learn. The me in the past couldn't deal with failure; not being the best wasn't good enough. However, going through my first year of high school to now, I began to realize that I don't have to perfect everything. Life is all about mistakes and if you make mistakes, then you should take things slowly and focus on the problems, in order to figure out what is wrong and overcome it. I wouldn't say my border is gone, but instead, it has been reduced. I still have trouble deciding important things such as future professions or whether or not to join a club. Another result of developing a new mindset is the realization that choices don't end your life. Back when I was still choosing my classes, I thought that once I had confirmed them, there would be no way out. However, I used my resources to find an alternative even when I felt like I was stuck. Unless you decide to choose to give up or purposely make bad decisions, then life should be fine. Don't ever give up, even when you feel like you don't have another option. You have control of your choices. Do what you think is right.

To the me in the future: don't give up. I know that you might be confused with what you want in life, but when you find your passion, stick with it. Your road will be hard and full of obstacles, but you can do it.

––––––––––

*Ryan Y. was born in San Francisco. He is currently fifteen years old. He has a mother, father, and a little sister who is one year younger than he is. He enjoys solving complex problems, along with gaming in his free time. At some point, he hopes to find something he is interested in and preferably expand on it.*

# GETTING CAUGHT

—

## HUGO Z.

It was a cloudy morning, and the classroom felt like a walk-in freezer due to the broken radiator that had probably been there since the school was first built. Mrs. Klein, my fourth-grade teacher, was barking at all of us, giving us orders to take out our homework from last night. Her voice boomed, filling every corner of the classroom. Throughout the entire classroom, everyone's heads perked up and they dropped everything they were doing. Immediately, everyone rustled through their backpacks, tossing papers everywhere, trying to find their homework that they had carelessly shoved in. Classmates were panicking and whispering to each other, attempting to get some last-minute homework done. Fortunately, I had finished my homework, so I dug it out of my folder and proudly placed it in the middle of my desk, feeling a sense of pride and accomplishment. I had nothing to worry about.

Suddenly out of nowhere, a crumpled up Post-It note hit the back of my head. I looked over my shoulder and saw my friend Ben frantically signaling me.

"Psst…Hugo," Ben quietly whispered. "Can you please pass me last night's math homework? I think I left it at home."

"Why? Why should I? Why should I risk being caught and waste my recess in Mrs. Klein's room? I won't get anything out of you copying," I replied.

"I'll give you my bag of chips later."

That quickly shut me up and I reluctantly handed over my homework to him. A bag of chips was worth about a hundred dollars and could save me from having to eat the horrendous school lunch.

"You have three minutes before I need it back."

I quickly looked over my shoulder as a lookout for Ben, making sure Mrs. Klein wouldn't come over to our side of the classroom anytime soon. After two minutes, Mrs. Klein started making her way down the aisle near where we sat. My hands started trembling and sweating, and I started tapping my pencil on my desk. It seemed like Ben was taking an eternity to copy a few simple math problems onto his paper.

"Here's your paper back. I'll give you the chips at lunch."

"You'd better…"

Suddenly, I felt a gush of warm wind blowing down my back. It felt as if someone was out of breath and desperately gasping for air. I slowly looked over my shoulder and saw Mrs. Klein's shadow cast over my body. I looked at her, and she stared right back into my eyes. Her arms were crossed and it seemed like she was about to rip me into pieces.

"So, Hugo. What did Ben just hand back to you?"

My face reddened to the color of a tomato as she snatched my paper from the palm of my hand. All my classmates and friends stopped what they were doing and stared at me. It felt as if someone turned up the thermostat to a hundred degrees. Beads of sweat fell off my forehead and landed onto my homework. The entire class was silent, waiting for me to give a response. My eyes wandered throughout the room to my friends, classmates, and especially to Ben.

"HUGO! FOCUS!" she shouted. "Why did Ben just hand you your own homework?"

I tried to make a quick comeback but I couldn't. I could say that my homework fell on the floor and Ben was being a nice friend helping me pick it up. *No*, I thought, *Mrs. Klein probably saw Ben copying and was going to make an example out of me to the entire class.*

"Uh…my homework?" I slowly answered.

"YOU KNOW WHAT I MEAN! STOP TRYING TO ACT SMART WITH ME!" she shouted.

She was losing her patience and it seemed like she was about to blow. I was hoping that she would throw me out the room to save me from the embarrassment of getting yelled at in front of all my friends. My classmates started snickering and whispering to each other, planning on sharing their version of the incident during recess. Over the shoulder of Mrs. Klein, I spotted Ben acting cool and pretending he wasn't involved in this entire mess.

"I let Ben borrow it because he said he needed help with a problem on yesterday's math homework," I nervously replied.

"Oh really?" she said.

She picked up Ben's paper and then snatched the paper out of my hands. She held them side by side in the air and quickly scanned both papers like a copy machine.

"It seems here that the answers are *exactly* the same. You said you were only helping him with one problem. This can't be a coincidence, can it?" Mrs. Klein said with a smug smile.

She knew she had caught me and that her instincts were correct. It seemed that she was trying to assert her dominance over me, making a lesson out of me to scare the other students into submission.

"Yes, Mrs. Klein…" I admitted. "I let Ben copy my homework."

"Both of you will not receive credit for last night's homework and will be staying in for recess," she said, proceeding to toss the two papers into the recycling bin. "You will also be getting a phone call home. Hopefully your parents will get you two to do your homework every day."

She continued on, checking other students' homework. I quickly turned my head and tracked down Ben, who seemed unmoved by the whole experience that just went down. He shrugged and went about with his business. He remained a good friend of mine, though I never let him "borrow" my homework ever again.

The bell rang, signaling that recess time had started. All my classmates grouped up with their friends and walked down to the yard together. Not getting my recess or my homework credit for last night didn't matter much to me. The thing that I was most worried about was the phone call home.

My mom was a typical Asian parent. She was a woman that enforced strict rules upon her children, making sure they succeeded in life. *How will she react when she finds out about this whole mess? Will I be forced to attend Saturday math classes at Kumon or have it after school every day? My parents have already threatened me with these punishments every time I did something wrong, but it's never happened. This time it could really happen.* I put my head down on the cold wooden table, continuing to stress about all the possible punishments my parents could give me while I heard laughter outside and my friends playing basketball.

The day blew by as I wasn't on task, mostly anxious and worrying about my punishment when I got home. The last bell of the school day rang and everyone quickly rushed out of the classroom.

I hopped off the bus and trudged toward my apartment building. I took the stairs slowly leading up to our apartment, attempting to avoid an unavoidable punishment.

A gigantic wooden door stood in front of my way. My dad shoved the keys aimlessly at the keyhole with one hand, while reading the mail with the other. I quickly thought up ideas about how to counteract all the responses my mom would give me. The door creaked open and I heard crackles and pops coming from the kitchen. I attempted to quickly run through the kitchen and be unnoticed by my mom.

"HUGO—come out here RIGHT NOW!" my mom shouted from the kitchen.

"I was only helping him. I didn't know he was going to copy me word for word."

"It doesn't matter what happened. It only matters that you learn your lesson," my mom responded.

Reluctantly, I opened the door to my room and slowly walked toward the smell of food coming from the kitchen. At this point, I'd given up and I was ready to receive whatever punishment was coming my way.

"Well…?" my mom said while stir-frying vegetables.

I spilled the beans and the truth came pouring out. My mom didn't show me any sympathy and kept quiet during my rambling about how none of it was my fault. She paused for a moment and turned toward me. She looked me in the eyes and continued what she was doing. I formed a fist with my hands making my knuckles turn white. During those few seconds, it felt like she sucked all the information out of me.

"Alright, here's the deal. No computer on Friday, and if I get a call again from your teacher, you can expect to have a busy weekend for the rest of the year. Is this understood?"

"Fine."

*I got off pretty easily,* I thought to myself. From that point on, I set up an invisible border, protecting my grades and friendships. This "border" has helped me from the time I made it, all the way to tenth grade, where I currently still use this border to this day.

My advice to those reading this is that you should think about all the possible outcomes of the situation, not just positive outcomes.

---

*Hugo Z.* was born in San Francisco. He is currently fifteen years old. He likes to read and play video games. One of his goals for the future is to get into UC Davis after high school. He currently goes to school at Galileo and loves history. His favorite types of food are spicy foods.

# TOMORROW IS A
# NEW DAY

—

## A GUIDE FOR EDUCATORS

## WRITING PROMPT

In Chapter 1 of his book *Always Running*, Luis J. Rodriguez describes his experience with borders:

*"We never stopped crossing borders. The Rio Grande (or Rio Bravo, which is what the Mexicans call it, giving the name a power 'Rio Grande' just doesn't have) was only the first of countless barriers set in our path.*

*We kept jumping hurdles, kept breaking from the constraints, kept evading the border guards of every new trek. It was a metaphor to fill our lives—that river, that first crossing, the mother of all crossings. The L.A. River, for example, became a new barrier, keeping the Mexicans in their neighborhoods over on the vast east side of the city for years, except for forays downtown. Schools provided other restrictions: Don't speak Spanish, don't be Mexican—you don't belong. Railroad tracks divided us from communities where white people lived, such as South Gate and Lynwood across from Watts. We were invisible people in a city which thrived on glitter, big screens, and big names, but this glamour contained none of our names, none of our faces.*

*The refrain 'this is not your country' echoed for a lifetime."*

Write a narrative, poem, or letter exploring the concept of borders in your life. A border could be:

- a physical border (between buildings, neighborhoods, cities, states, countries, etc.)
- a division between people/languages/cultures
- a barrier (to understanding, communicating, doing something you want to do, etc.)
- a boundary you set to protect yourself or stand up against something
- an internal disconnect (between different aspects of your identity, between how you feel and what you express, between you and your emotions)

**GUIDING QUESTIONS:**

What is the border? How does it function? What does it look like, feel like, etc. What type of border is it (solid, permeable, invisible, or something else)?

- When did you first become aware of this "border"?
- Is the border permanent? Temporary? Who made it? Why is it there?
- How does this "border" impact you and who you are in the world?

### Genre Options

- *Narrative:* Tell a story of a moment in time when the border was prominent in your life.
- *Letter:* Write to someone impacted by the border or from the perspective of someone impacted.
- *Extension activity:* Write a response to your first letter.
- *Poem:* Write a poem exploring the border(s) you identified.

## INTERACTIVE ACTIVITIES TO
## PAIR WITH *WE ALL BELONG*

———

**MAKING CONNECTIONS:** Choose a piece of writing to read together as a class. As they read, students will actively annotate the text with connections to themselves, other texts, and the world. *What does this piece remind you of? Can you relate to the narrator? What images come to mind as you read? How is it similar to other stories you have read, heard, or watched? What local and global issues are raised? How does the narrative connect to history, current events, and the future?* Start with modeling and guided practice of the strategy, and then transition to independent work. Student responses can then be synthesized in a discussion or through writing.

**SOCRATIC DIALOGUE:** Choose a piece of writing to read together as a class and use that as a springboard to explore the questions listed above. Have students then identify textual evidence to support their stance on the selected theme question to prepare for the discussion. The dialogue can occur between a pair of students, as a fishbowl, or you can split the class to present and defend opposing views. The teacher or students can act as facilitators. Establish norms for participation. Consider the following open-ended questions to start, or create your own that are specific to the text: *What is the piece saying about the selected "border"? How does the piece's outcome support your claim? What are other points of view?*

**DRAMATIZE IT:** Assign a group of students to a scene or scenes, and ask them to write a play based on the narrative. Ask students to create additional text, like character and scene descriptions, stage directions, and design. Invite students to act out their plays, or film their dramatization and share it with others.

**WRITE WHAT HAPPENS NEXT:** Starting with a piece of writing that ends unresolved, allow students to adopt and extend the narrative. Invite them to pick up where the author left off, and write what might happen next, based on what they know about the characters and plot. Students are welcome to write multiple possible endings, and reflect on the strengths and limitations of each.

**CREATE A GRAPHIC REPRESENTATION:** Incorporating a visual element is helpful to both plan and process. In developing the pieces in this book, many students utilized plot maps in order to flesh out their ideas and to stay on track. For this activity, have students choose a narrative to interpret visually—in graphic novel form, via photography, or through another visual medium—in order to see the piece from a fresh perspective and bring it to life in a new way.

**DEBATE THE BORDER:** Read the foreword and the following response by Luis J. Rodriguez from PBS's P.O.V. border talk:

*P.O.V.* When and how are borders useful?

*Luis:* I believe we have long outlived and outused borders in this world. Perhaps at one time they were necessary—but today they are the source of most conflicts and war in the world for at least the past 3,000 years (included in this are the world's religions, another major source of conflict and war in the world). Who needs them? We have advanced to a level where we can share the earth's resources with everyone (proper and respectful relationship so that these resources are not depleted). No more hunger. No more exiled and homeless. No more class society where the rich feed off the poor (there is no other way they can stay rich). We can live in a world where everyone is valued and everyone's unique gifts, attributes, propensities, and talents are essential to a full and vibrant community. If we can dream it, we can realize it. Of course, society would have to be reorganized along completely different lines—

not for profit, power and establishing borders. And why not? We've suffered enough by the work of our own hand—it's time to finish this business of borders.

Ask students to complete a writing assignment first. Do you agree or disagree with Luis's assessment that we've "outlived and out-used" borders? Why or why not? How might we reimagine a society without borders? Next, conduct a debate. Call on students with different views to explain their stance. Students will then select a statement that they had a strong reaction to (positive or negative) and read the part aloud.

## CONTENT STANDARDS

—

This project-based unit was designed to address a broad array of standards in English Language Arts. The following are key standards as addressed in the ninth and tenth grade common core. This unit can be adapted to target many English Language Arts standards for other grade levels if needed.

### READING

*CCSS.ELA-Literacy.RL.9-10.1*
Cite strong and thorough textual evidence to support analysis of what the text says explicitly as well as inferences drawn from the text.

*CCSS.ELA-Literacy.RL.9-10.2*
Determine a theme or central idea of a text and analyze in detail its development over the course of the text, including how it emerges and is shaped and refined by specific details; provide an objective summary of the text.

*CCSS.ELA-Literacy.RL.9-10.3*
Analyze how complex characters (e.g., those with multiple or conflicting motivations) develop over the course of a text, interact with other characters, and advance the plot or develop the theme.

*CCSS.ELA-LITERACY.RL.9-10.4*
Determine the meaning of words and phrases as they are used in the text, including figurative and connotative meanings; analyze the cumulative impact of specific word choices on meaning and tone (e.g., how the language evokes a sense of time and place; how it sets a formal or informal tone).

*CCSS.ELA-LITERACY.RL.9-10.5*

Analyze how an author's choices concerning how to structure a text, order events within it (e.g., parallel plots), and manipulate time (e.g., pacing, flashbacks) create such effects as mystery, tension, or surprise.

*CCSS.ELA-LITERACY.RL.9-10.6*

Analyze a particular point of view or cultural experience reflected in a work of literature from outside the United States, drawing on a wide reading of world literature.

## WRITING

*CCSS.ELA-LITERACY.W.9-10.3*

Write narratives to develop real or imagined experiences or events using effective technique, well-chosen details, and well-structured event sequences.

*CCSS.ELA-LITERACY.W.9-10.3.A*

Engage and orient the reader by setting out a problem, situation, or observation, establishing one or multiple point(s) of view, and introducing a narrator and/or characters; create a smooth progression of experiences or events.

*CCSS.ELA-LITERACY.W.9-10.3.B*

Use narrative techniques, such as dialogue, pacing, description, reflection, and multiple plot lines, to develop experiences, events, and/or characters.

*CCSS.ELA-LITERACY.W.9-10.3.C*

Use a variety of techniques to sequence events so that they build on one another to create a coherent whole.

### CCSS.ELA-LITERACY.W.9-10.3.D

Use precise words and phrases, telling details, and sensory language to convey a vivid picture of the experiences, events, setting, and/or characters.

### CCSS.ELA-LITERACY.W.9-10.3.E

Provide a conclusion that follows from and reflects on what is experienced, observed, or resolved over the course of the narrative.

### CCSS.ELA-LITERACY.W.9-10.4

Produce clear and coherent writing in which the development, organization, and style are appropriate to task, purpose, and audience.

### CCSS.ELA-LITERACY.W.9-10.5

Develop and strengthen writing as needed by planning, revising, editing, rewriting, or trying a new approach, focusing on addressing what is most significant for a specific purpose and audience.

### CCSS.ELA-LITERACY.W.9-10.10

Write routinely over extended time frames (time for research, reflection, and revision) and shorter time frames (a single sitting or a day or two) for a range of tasks, purposes, and audiences.

## SPEAKING AND LISTENING

### CCSS.ELA-LITERACY.SL.9-10.1

Initiate and participate effectively in a range of collaborative discussions (one-on-one, in groups, and teacher-led) with diverse partners on grades 9-10 topics, texts, and issues, building on others' ideas and expressing their own clearly and persuasively.

### CCSS.ELA-LITERACY.SL.9-10.1.A

Come to discussions prepared, having read and researched material under study; explicitly draw on that preparation by referring to evidence from texts and other research on the topic or issue to stimulate a thoughtful, well-reasoned exchange of ideas.

### CCSS.ELA-LITERACY.SL.9-10.1.B

Work with peers to set rules for collegial discussions and decision-making (e.g., informal consensus, taking votes on key issues, presentation of alternate views), clear goals and deadlines, and individual roles as needed.

### CCSS.ELA-LITERACY.SL.9-10.1.C

Propel conversations by posing and responding to questions that relate the current discussion to broader themes or larger ideas; actively incorporate others into the discussion; and clarify, verify, or challenge ideas and conclusions.

### CCSS.ELA-LITERACY.SL.9-10.1.D

Respond thoughtfully to diverse perspectives, summarize points of agreement and disagreement, and, when warranted, qualify or justify their own views and understanding and make new connections in light of the evidence and reasoning presented.

### CCSS.ELA-LITERACY.SL.9-10.2

Integrate multiple sources of information presented in diverse media or formats (e.g., visually, quantitatively, orally) evaluating the credibility and accuracy of each source.

### CCSS.ELA-LITERACY.SL.9-10.3

Evaluate a speaker's point of view, reasoning, and use of evidence and rhetoric, identifying any fallacious reasoning or exaggerated or distorted evidence.

*CCSS.ELA-LITERACY.SL.9-10.4*

Present information, findings, and supporting evidence clearly, concisely, and logically such that listeners can follow the line of reasoning, and the organization, development, substance, and style are appropriate to purpose, audience, and task.

*CCSS.ELA-LITERACY.W.9-10.3.A*

Engage and orient the reader by setting out a problem, situation, or observation, establishing one or multiple point(s) of view, and introducing a narrator and/or characters; create a smooth progression of experiences or events.

## EDUCATOR RESOURCES
—

*Don't Forget to Write* (2005) contains fifty-four of the best lesson plans used in workshops taught at 826 Valencia, 826NYC, and 826LA, giving away all of our secrets for making writing fun. Each lesson plan was written by its original workshop teacher, including Jonathan Ames, Aimee Bender, Dave Eggers, Erika Lopez, Julie Orringer, Jon Scieszka, Sarah Vowell, and many others. If you are a parent or a teacher, this book is meant to make your life easier, as it contains enthralling and effective ideas to get your students writing. It can also be used as a resource for the aspiring writer. In 2011, 826 National published a two-volume second edition of *Don't Forget to Write,* also available in our stores.

*STEM to Story* (2015) contains dynamic lesson plans that use hands-on discovery and creative writing to teach students about science, technology, math, and engineering. These quirky, exploratory lessons are sure to awaken the imagination and ignite passions for both STEM and creative writing. *STEM to Story* is a boon to teachers, parents, and students alike, as each lesson plan is aligned with Common Core and Next Gen Science Standards.

# OTHER BOOKS FROM
# 826 VALENCIA
—

826 Valencia produces a variety of publications, each of which contains work written by students in our programs. Some are professionally printed and nationally distributed; others are glued together on-site and sold in our stores. These projects represent some of the most exciting work at 826 Valencia, as they enable Bay Area students to experience a world of publishing not otherwise available to them. The following is a selection of publications available for purchase at our stores, online at 826valencia.org/store, or through your local bookstore.

*The Battle Within (2018)* is a collection of writing from the students of Ida B. Wells High School in San Francisco. Inspired by the themes in Khaled Hosseini's *The Kite Runner*, these young authors crafted powerful stories, poems, and letters that get to the heart of what it means to struggle, to regret, to overcome, to love. We invite you to take a moment to step inside each one of their stories, to read their words, and to consider their hopes.

*We Are Here, Walking Toward the Unknown (2017)* is a collection of narrative essays about adapting, written by students at Phillip & Sala Burton Academic High School. Have you ever been misunderstood or judged? What fears are you working to overcome? Can science and technology go too far? If you had the opportunity to go back, how would you fix a past mistake? While these questions were inspired by the themes in Mary Shelley's *Frankenstein*, a book written in the nineteenth century, they are still as thought-provoking and relevant as ever. In this collection, the seniors of Burton High in San Francisco set out to answer them in the form of personal narratives, fictional short stories, and letters. From intimate reflections about their own lived experiences, to the development of creative and futuristic worlds, these young authors meditate on our past, present, and future—and the results prove illuminating for all.

*Walk the Earth in Our Shoes and Plant Some Seeds Behind You* *(2016)* collects personal essays from students at John O'Connell High School. What would we learn if we could interview a whale? Is diversity as advantageous in a social community as it is in a coral reef? How does our environment affect us, and how do we affect our environment? These questions are both age-old and urgent, and in this collection, ninth- and tenth-grade authors set out to answer them. From how their neighborhoods are changing, to what it's like to live in a drought, these young authors share their views and experiences as they investigate the way ecosystems work—and their answers hold insights everyone should read.

*If the World Only Knew (2015)* is a collection of essays written by sixty-six ninth graders at Mission High School. In this book students reflect on their beliefs and where they come from—the people who imparted them, the times when they were most necessary, and the ways in which the world has tested them. The collection is a testament to the power of personal conviction, and a powerful case for why young peoples' voices should be heard—and believed.

*Uncharted Places (2014)* is a collection of essays by fifty-two juniors and seniors at Thurgood Marshall High School that examines the idea of "place" and what it means to these young authors. It contains stories about locales real and imagined, internal and external, places of transition and those of comfort. These young writers bravely share their views of the world, giving us a glimpse into the places that are most important to them—those not necessarily found on a map, but in the heart.

*Beyond Stolen Flames, Forbidden Fruit, and Telephone Booths (2011)* is a collection of essays and short stories, written by fifty-three juniors and seniors at June Jordan School for Equity, in which young writers explore the role of myth in our world today. Students wrote pieces of fiction and nonfiction, retelling old myths, creating new ones, celebrating everyday heroes, and recognizing the tales that their families have told over and over. With a foreword by Khaled Hosseini, the result is a collection with a powerful message about the stories that have shaped students' perspectives and the world they know.

*I Live Real Close to Where You Used to Live (2010)* is a collection of letters to Michelle, Sasha, Malia, and Bo Obama written by students across the 826 network. These letters are packed with questions, advice, and the occasional request to be invited over to the White House for dinner.

*Show of Hands (2009)* is a collection of stories and essays written by fifty-four juniors and seniors at Mission High School. It amplifies the students' voices as they reflect on one of humanity's most revered guides for moral behavior: the Golden Rule, which tells us that we should act toward others as we would want them to act toward us. Whether speaking about global issues, street violence, or the way to behave among friends and family, the voices of these young essayists are brilliant, thoughtful, and, most of all, urgent.

*Thanks and Have Fun Running the Country (2009)* is a collection of letters penned by our After-School Tutoring students to newly-elected President Obama. In this collection, which arrived at inauguration time, there's loads of advice for the president—often hilarious, sometimes heartfelt, and occasionally downright practical. The letters have been featured in *the New York Times,* the *San Francisco Chronicle,* and on *This American Life.*

*Exactly (2007)* is a hardbound book of colorful stories for children ages nine to eleven. This collection of fifty-six narratives by students at Raoul Wallenberg Traditional High School is illustrated by forty-three professional artists. It passes on lessons that teenagers want the next generation to know.

*Home Wasn't Built in a Day (2006)* is a collection of short stories based on family myths and legends. With a foreword by actor and comedian Robin Williams, the book comes alive through powerful student voices that explore just what it is that makes a house a home.

# A THANK YOU LETTER FROM THE EDITOR

—

## ACKNOWLEDGMENTS

The Young Authors' Book Project (YABP) is an annual labor of love that relies heavily on the generosity and dedication of an incredible number of people. This year was no exception. Our 2019 YABP by the numbers: one school, five weeks, ten sessions, three editorial board meetings, forty volunteers, fifty students, and countless hours of editing. It's been a journey, from start to finish, and we are deeply grateful for all of the support.

We'd first like to thank the school community at Galileo High School for being such a welcoming collaborator for this project. We'd especially like to thank Galileo Principal Tami Benau for welcoming 826 Valencia and other great resources for students into her school. Thank you also to the staff, administrators, and students who make Galileo such a great place to be.

We are honored to have worked with two incredible partner teachers on this project, Kristy Morrison and Jennifer Stangland. Ms. Morrison and Ms. Stangland are outstanding educators in every way; they know their students well and celebrate them as they push them to succeed, work tirelessly to ensure that everyone has access to the greatest support and most authentic opportunities possible, and inspire confidence and enthusiasm among all who set foot in their classrooms. For these reasons and more, Ms. Morrison and Ms. Stangland were dream collaborators for this project. We look forward to seeing the many ways in which their students will carry the skills and confidence they've gained in their classes with them as they move through the world.

We owe Luis J. Rodriguez a tremendous debt of gratitude for his engagement throughout the entire Young Authors' Book Project. From the moment we connected with Luis, he has greeted every request and every opportunity we have presented with a resounding yes and a relentlessly positive attitude. When he visited the students at Galileo High School after the final tutoring session, he captivated the room of young authors with his advice about writing and life. Mr. Rodriguez provided encouraging and candid responses to all of the questions students posed—from reflections about his own experiences in life, to advice for young writers, to more philosophical discussions about the concept of borders.

With Luis J. Rodriguez's engagement in the project, students saw their school assignment transform into a powerful work of literature. And in his foreword, he captured the energy in all the students' pieces and helped pull together and introduce all the ways they understand that *We All Belong*. We truly cannot thank Luis enough.

A small group of students and volunteer tutors took their dedication to this book above and beyond by continuing to hand-edit each of the narratives collected here, and to set the editorial direction for the book. The editorial board showed great professionalism and growth over the course of this process. In just three weeks, these students went from authors to co-editors, and in doing so they gained confidence in their writing skills and became empowered to make the big decisions that made this book a reality. Their hard work shines on these pages. As such, we'd like to extend a special thanks to these students: Kevin G., Florante M., Jaedyn N., Elizabeth W., Caiyan Y. and these volunteers: Susannah Cohen, Geordi Galang, Cristina Giner, Eric Hendrickson, Maura Kealey, Caroline Moon.

Enormous thanks to Molly Schellenger, the designer of this book, for honoring the young authors' words by giving them such a beautiful home! A huge thank you to Lisa Congdon for illustrating this book, bringing our students' writing to life and so beautifully representing their ideas in the cover art. To Brad Amorosino, our Design Director, and Meghan Ryan, our Publications Manager, thank you both for your invaluable work on this publication, for amplifying the students' voices with your design expertise and for keeping us all on deadline. Huge thanks to Beret Olsen, our copyeditor whose super-human eyes catch every single extra space and misplaced comma, for lending your time to helping our young authors' words shine.

Finally, we are so proud of the young writers collected here. Writers, for sharing your unique and poignant perspectives with us, for your courage in offering your stories and voices to the world, and for never giving up on the writing process, we commend and profoundly thank you.

Ryan Young
*Programs Manager and Editor*

# ABOUT 826 VALENCIA

—

## WHO WE ARE AND WHAT WE DO

—

826 Valencia is a nonprofit organization dedicated to supporting under-resourced students ages six to eighteen with their creative and expository writing skills and to helping teachers inspire their students to write. Our services are structured around the understanding that great leaps in learning can happen with one-on-one attention and that strong writing skills are fundamental to future success.

826 Valencia comprises three writing centers—located in San Francisco's Mission District, Tenderloin neighborhood, and Mission Bay—and three satellite classrooms at nearby schools. All of our centers are fronted by kid-friendly, weird, and whimsical stores, which serve as portals to learning and gateways for the community. All of our programs are offered free of charge. Since we first opened our doors in 2002, thousands of volunteers have dedicated their time to working with tens of thousands of students.

## PROGRAMS

—

**FIELD TRIPS** Classes from public schools around San Francisco visit our writing centers for a morning of high-energy learning about the craft of storytelling. Four days a week, our Field Trips produce bound, illustrated books and professional-quality podcasts, infusing creativity, collaboration, and the arts into students' regular school day.

**IN-SCHOOLS PROGRAMS** We bring teams of volunteers into high-need schools around the city to support teachers and provide one-on-one assistance to students as they tackle various writing projects, including newspapers, research papers, oral histories, and more. We have a special presence at Buena Vista Horace Mann K–8, Everett Middle School, and Mission High School, where we staff dedicated Writers' Rooms throughout the school year.

**AFTER-SCHOOL TUTORING** During the school year, 826 Valencia's centers are packed five days a week with neighborhood students who come in after school and in the evenings for tutoring in all subject areas, with a special emphasis on creative writing and publishing. During the summer, these students participate in our five-week Exploring Words Summer Camp, where we explore science and writing through projects, outings, and activities in a super fun educational environment.

**WORKSHOPS** 826 Valencia offers workshops designed to foster creativity and strengthen writing skills in a wide variety of areas, from playwriting to personal essays to starting a zine. All workshops, from the playful to the practical, are project-based and are taught by experienced, accomplished professionals. Over the summer, our Young Authors' Workshop provides a two-week intensive writing experience for high-school-age students.

**COLLEGE AND CAREER READINESS** We offer a roster of programs designed to help students get into college and be successful there. Every year, we grant six $15,000 scholarships to college-bound seniors, provide one-on-one support to two hundred students via the Great San Francisco Personal Statement Weekend, and partner with ScholarMatch to offer college access workshops to the middle school and high school students in our tutoring programs. We also offer internships, peer tutoring stipends, and career workshops to our youth leaders.

**PUBLISHING** Students in all of 826 Valencia's programs have the ability to explore, experience, and celebrate themselves as writers in part because of our professional-quality publishing. In addition to the book you're holding, 826 Valencia publishes newspapers, magazines, chapbooks, podcasts, and blogs—all written by students.

**TEACHER OF THE MONTH** From the beginning, 826 Valencia's goal has been to support teachers. We aim both to provide the classroom support that helps our hardworking teachers meet the needs of all our students and to celebrate their important work. Every month, we receive letters from students, parents, and educators nominating outstanding teachers for our Teacher of the Month award, which comes with a $1,500 honorarium. Know an SFUSD teacher you want to nominate? Guidelines can be found at 826valencia.org.

## PEOPLE

—

### STAFF

Bita Nazarian *Executive Director*

Brad Amorosino *Design Director*
Melissa Anguiano *Programs Coordinator*
Dana Belott *Programs Coordinator*
Nana Boateng *Programs Coordinator*
Angelina Brand *Programs Coordinator*
Nicole C. Brown *Director of Individual Philanthropy*
Sarah Bruhns *Development Coordinator*
Karla Brundage *Programs Manager*
Ricardo Cruz-Chong *Programs Coordinator*
Lila Cutter *Volunteer Engagement Coordinator*
Precediha Dangerfield *Programs Coordinator*
Shelby Dale DeWeese *Programs Coordinator*
Allyson Halpern *Advancement Director*
Virdell Hickman *Operations Manager*
Juan Ibarra *Interns Manager*
Caroline Kangas *Stores Director*
Kavitha Lotun *Volunteer Engagement Manager*
Montana Manalo *Design Associate*
Molly Parent *Communications Manager*

Christina V. Perry *Director of Education*
Kathleen Rodríguez *Programs Manager*
Meghan Ryan *Publications Manager*
Sendy Santamaria *Design Associate*
Ashley Smith *Programs Manager*
Hai Lun Tan *Programs Coordinator*
Leah Tarlen *Director of Institutional Gifts*
Jillian Wasick *Programs Director*
Byron Weiss *Stores Manager*
Ryan Young *Programs Manager*
Gene Yuson *Director, Human Resources*

## AMERICORPS SUPPORT STAFF THROUGH SUMMER 2019

Paolo Bicchieri *Volunteer Associate*
Alexandra Cotrim *In-Schools Programs Associate*
Paloma Mariz *Communications Associate*
Lucie Pereira *Field Trips and After-School Tutoring Associate*
Stina Perkins *Tenderloin Programs Associate*
Alex Phipps *Development and Evaluations Associate*
Shelby Urbina *Buena Vista Horace Mann Programs Associate*

## STORE STAFF

Kanya Abe
Tran Bao
Isabel Craik
Megan Gamino
Steven Gomez
Jonathan Kendall
Tim Ratanpreuskul
Angelina Sideris
Denise Smith

**BOARD OF DIRECTORS**
Eric Abrams
Colleen Quinn Amster
Joya Banerjee
Lisa Brown
Carolyn Feinstein Edwards
Alex Lerner
Jim Lesser
Julia Matsudaira
Enikia Ford Morthel
Dave Pell
Joe Vasquez
Rachel Swain Yeaman

**CO-FOUNDERS**
Nínive Calegari
Dave Eggers

**OUR VOLUNTEERS** There's absolutely no way we could create hundreds of publications and serve thousands of students annually without a legion of volunteers. These incredible people work in all realms, from tutoring to fundraising and beyond. They range in age, background and expertise but all have a shared passion for our work with young people. Volunteers past and present, you know who you are. Thank you, thank you, thank you.

**826 NATIONAL** 826 Valencia's success has spread across the country. Under the umbrella of 826 National, writing and tutoring centers have opened up in six more cities. If you would like to learn more about other 826 programs, please visit the following websites.

826 National
826national.org

826 Boston
826boston.org

826CHI
826chi.org

826DC
826dc.org

826LA
826la.org

826michigan
826michigan.org

826 New Orleans
826neworleans.org

826NYC
826nyc.org

826 Valencia
826valencia.org

# IT'S ALWAYS A GOOD
# TIME TO GIVE

—

**WE NEED YOUR HELP**

We could not do this work without the thousands of volunteers who make our programs possible. We are always seeking more volunteer tutors, and volunteers with design, illustration, photography, and audio editing skills. It's easy to become a volunteer and a bunch of fun to actually do it.

Please fill out our online application to let us know how you'd like to lend your time:

**826valencia.org/volunteer**

**OTHER WAYS TO GIVE**

Whether it's loose change or heaps of cash, a donation of any size will help 826 Valencia continue to offer a variety of free writing and publishing programs to Bay Area youth.

Please make a donation at:

**826valencia.org/donate**

You can also mail your contribution to:

**826 Valencia Street, San Francisco, CA 94110**

*Your donation is tax-deductible. What a plus! Thank you!*